THE GUARDIANS *of* GA'HOOLE

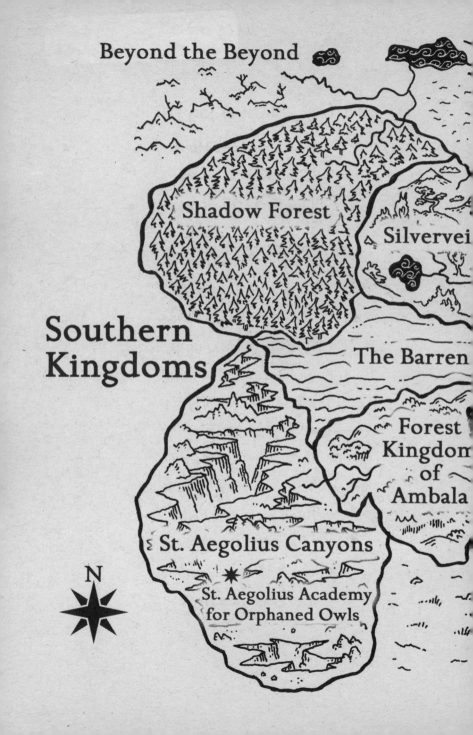

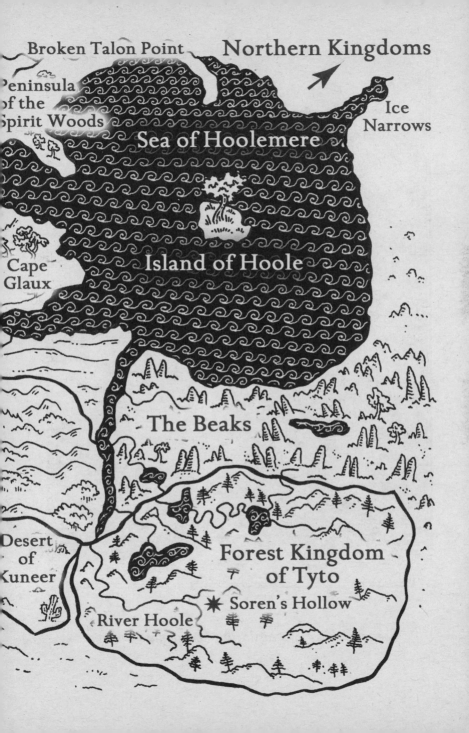

Soon the walls of the castle ruins rose in the dawn mist.

GUARDIANS
of GA'HOOLE

BOOK THREE

The Rescue

BY KATHRYN LASKY

SCHOLASTIC INC.

New York Toronto London Auckland
Sydney Mexico City New Delhi Hong Kong

ISBN 978-0-439-40559-1

Artwork by Richard Cowdrey
Design by Steve Scott

15 14 13 12 11 10 9 8 7 6 5 4 3 2 1   10 11 12 13 14 15/0

Printed in the U.S.A.   40

First printing, January 2004

Northern Kingdoms

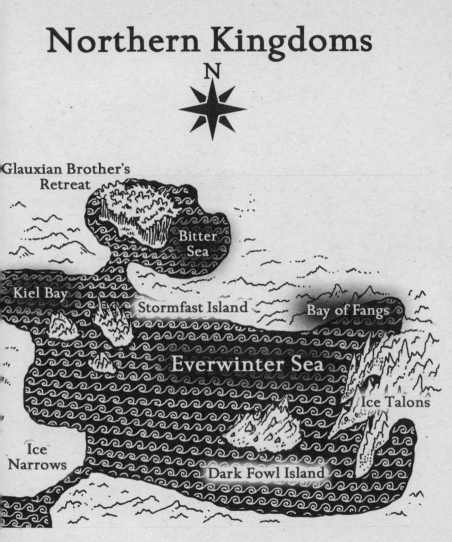

Glauxian Brother's Retreat

Bitter Sea

Kiel Bay

Stormfast Island

Bay of Fangs

Everwinter Sea

Ice Talons

Ice Narrows

Dark Fowl Island

Southern Kingdoms

Contents

CHAPTER ONE

Blood Dawn

The tail of the comet slashed the dawn and in the red light of the rising sun, for a brief instant, it seemed as if the comet was bleeding across the sky. Every other owl had already tucked into their hollows in the Great Ga'Hoole Tree for the day's sleep. Every owl, that is, except for Soren, who perched on the highest limb of this tallest Ga'Hoole tree on earth. He scoured the horizon for a sign, any sign of his beloved teacher, Ezylryb.

Ezylryb had disappeared almost two months before. The old Whiskered Screech, indeed the oldest teacher, or "ryb" as they were called, of the great tree had flown out on a mission that late summer night to help rescue owlets from what was now referred to as the Great Downing. Scores of young orphan owlets had mysteriously been found scattered on the ground, some mortally wounded, others stunned and incoherent. None of them had been found anywhere near their nests, but in an open field that for the most part could boast no trees with hollows. It was a complete mystery as to how these young owlets, most of whom could barely fly, had gotten there. It was as if they had simply dropped out of the night sky. And one of those owlets had been Soren's sister, Eglantine.

After Soren himself had been shoved from his nest by his brother, Kludd, nearly a year before, and subsequently captured by the violent and depraved owls of St. Aggie's, he had lost all hope of ever seeing his sister or his parents again. Even after he had escaped St. Aggie's with his best friend Gylfie, a little Elf Owl who had also been captured, he had still dared not to really hope. But then Eglantine had been found by two other dear friends: Twilight, the Great Gray, and Digger, the Burrowing Owl, both of whom had flown out with others on the night of the Great Downing on countless search-and-rescue missions. And Ezylryb, who rarely left the tree except for his responsibilities as leader of the weather interpretation and the colliering chaws, had flown out in an attempt to unravel the strange occurrences of that night. But he had never returned.

It seemed grossly unfair to Soren that once he had finally gotten his sister back, his favorite ryb had vanished. Maybe that was a selfish way to think but he couldn't help it. Soren felt that most of what he knew he had learned from the gruff old Whiskered Screech Owl. Ezylryb was not what anyone would call pretty to look at, with one eye held in a perpetual squint, his left foot mangled to the point of missing one talon, and a low voice that sounded like something between a growl and distant thunder — no, Ezylryb wasn't exactly appealing.

"An acquired taste," Gylfie had said. Well, Soren had certainly acquired the taste.

As a member of both the weather interpretation and the colliering chaws, which flew into forest fires to gather coals for the forge of Bubo the blacksmith, Soren had learned his abilities directly from the master. And though Ezylryb was a stern master, often grouchy and suffering no nonsense, he was, of all the rybs, the most fiercely devoted to his students and his chaw members.

The chaws were the small teams into which the owls were organized. In the chaws, they learned a particular skill that was vital to the survival of not just the owls of Ga'Hoole but to all the kingdoms of owls. Ezylryb led two chaws — weathering and colliering. But for all his gruff ways, he was certainly not above cracking a joke — sometimes very dirty jokes, much to the horror of Otulissa, a Spotted Owl, who was just Soren's age and quite prim and proper and was given to airs. Otulissa was always carrying on about her ancient and distinguished ancestors. One of her favorite words was "appalling." She was constantly being "appalled" by Ezylryb's "crudeness," his "lack of refinement," his "coarse ways." And Ezylryb was constantly telling Otulissa to "give it a blow." This was the most impolite way an owl could tell another to shut up. The two bickered constantly, and yet Otulissa had turned into a good chaw member and that was all that really counted to Ezylryb.

But now there was no more bickering. No more crude jokes. No more climbing the baggywrinkles, flying upside down in the gutter, punching the wind and popping the scuppers, doing the hurly burly and all the wonderful maneuvers the owls did when they flew through gales and storms and even hurricanes in the weather interpretation chaw. Life seemed flat without Ezylryb, the night less black, the stars dull, even as this comet, like a great raw gash in the sky, ripped apart the dawn.

"Some say a comet's an omen." Soren felt the branch he was perched on quiver. "Octavia!" The fat old nest-maid snake slithered out onto the branch. "What are you doing out here?" Soren asked.

"Same thing as you. Looking for Ezylryb." She sighed. But, of course, Octavia, like all nest-maid snakes, who tidied up the hollows of owls and kept them free of vermin, was blind. In fact, she had no eyes, just two small indentations where eyes should be. But nest-maids were renowned for their extraordinary sensory skills. They could hear and feel things that other creatures could not. So, if there were wing beats out there, wing beats that had the sound peculiar to those of Ezylryb, she would know. Although owls were silent fliers, each stirred the air with its wings in a unique fashion that only a nest-maid snake could detect. And Octavia, with her musical background and years in the harp guild under Madame Plonk's guidance, was especially keen to all sorts of vibrations.

The harp guild was one of the most prestigious of all the guilds for which the blind nest-maid snakes were chosen to belong. Dear Mrs. Plithiver, who had served in Soren's family's hollow and with whom he had been miraculously reunited, was also a member of this guild. The snakes wove themselves in and out of the harp's strings, playing the accompaniment for Madame Plonk, the beautiful Snowy Owl with the shimmering voice. Octavia had served as a nest-maid for Madame Plonk and Ezylryb. Indeed, she and Ezylryb had arrived at the Great Ga'Hoole Tree together from the land of the North Waters of the Northern Kingdoms years and years ago. She was completely devoted to Ezylryb and, although she had never said much about how she and the old Screech Owl had first met, there were rumors that she had been rescued by Ezylryb and that she, unlike the other snakes, had not been born blind. Something had happened to make her go blind. She certainly did not have the same rosy scales as the other snakes. She was instead a pale greenish blue.

The old snake sighed again.

"I just don't understand," Soren said. "He's too smart to get lost."

Octavia shook her head. "I don't think he's lost, Soren." Soren swung his head around to look at her. *Then what does she think? Does she think he is dead?* Octavia said very little these days. It was almost as if she was afraid to speculate on the fate of her beloved master. The others, Barran and Boron, the monarchs of the great tree, speculated constantly, as did Strix Struma, another revered teacher. But the creature who knew Ezylryb the best and the longest offered no such speculations, no ideas, and yet Soren felt she did know something that truly scared her. Something so horrible as to be unspeakable. Thus, her seemingly impenetrable silences. Soren felt this about Octavia, he felt it in his gizzard where all owls sensed their strongest feelings and experienced their most powerful intuitions. Could he share this with someone? Who? Otulissa? Never. Twilight? Not Twilight. He was too action-oriented. Maybe Gylfie, his best friend, but Gylfie was too practical. She liked definite evidence, and was a stickler for words. Soren could imagine Gylfie pushing if he said that he felt Octavia knew something: *What do you mean by "know"?*

"You better get along, young'un," Octavia said. "Time for you to sleep. I can feel the sun. The dawn's getting old."

"Can you feel the comet, too?" Soren asked suddenly.

"Ooh." It was more like a soft groan or a whispering exhalation. "I don't know." But she did know. Soren knew it. She felt it, and it worried her. He shouldn't have asked, and yet he could not stop himself from asking more. "Do you believe it really is an omen like some say?"

"Who is some?" she asked sharply. "I haven't heard anyone in the tree nattering on about omens."

"What about you? I heard you just a few minutes ago."

Octavia paused. "Listen, Soren, I'm just a fat old snake from the Northern Kingdoms, the country of the North Waters. We're a naturally suspicious lot. So don't you pay me any heed. Now flutter back down to your hollow."

"Yes, ma'am," Soren replied. It didn't pay to upset a nest-maid snake.

So the young Barn Owl swooped down through the spreading branches of the Great Ga'Hoole Tree to the hollow he shared with his sister, Eglantine, and his best friends, Gylfie, Twilight, and Digger. As he flew, looping through the limbs, he saw the sun rise fierce and bright. As clouds the color of blood crouched on the horizon, a ter-

7

rible apprehension coursed through Soren's hollow bones and set his gizzard aquiver.

Digger! Why had he never thought of sharing his feelings about Octavia with Digger? Soren blinked as he stepped into the dim light of the hollow and saw the sleeping shapes of his best friends. Digger was a very odd owl in every sense of the word. For starters, he had lived his entire life — until he was orphaned — not in a tree but a burrow. With his long, strong, featherless legs, he had preferred walking to flying when Soren and Gylfie and Twilight first met him. He had planned to walk all the way across the desert in search of his parents until mortal danger intervened and the three owls convinced him otherwise. Nervous and high-strung, Digger worried a lot but, at the same time, this owl was a very deep thinker. He was always asking the strangest questions. Boron said that Digger possessed what he called a "philosophical turn of mind." Soren wasn't sure what that meant exactly. He only knew that if he said to Digger, "I think Octavia might know something about Ezylryb," Digger, unlike Gylfie, would go deeper. He would not be just a stickler for words or, like Twilight, say, "Well, what are you going to do about it?"

Soren wished he could wake Digger up right now and

share his thoughts. But he didn't want to risk waking the others. No, he would just have to wait until they all rose at First Black.

And so Soren squashed himself into the corner bed of soft moss and down. He stole a glance at Digger before he drifted off. Digger, unlike the others, did not sleep standing or sometimes perched, but in a curious posture that more or less could be described as a squat supported by his short stubby tail with his legs splayed out to the sides. *Good Glaux, that owl even sleeps odd.* That was Soren's last thought before he drifted off to sleep.

CHAPTER TWO

Flecks in the Night!

The dawn bled into night, flaying the darkness, turning the black red, and Soren, with Digger by his side, flew through it.

"Strange isn't it, Soren, how even at night the comet makes this color?"

"I know. And look at those sparks from the tail just below the moon. Great Glaux, even the moon is beginning to look red." Digger's voice was quavery with worry.

"I told you about Octavia. How she thinks it's an omen, or at least I think she thinks it is, even though she won't really admit it."

"Why won't she admit it?" Digger asked.

"I think she's sensitive about coming from the great North Waters. She says everyone there is very superstitious, but I don't know, I guess she just thinks the owls here will laugh at her or something. I'm not sure."

Suddenly, Soren was experiencing a tight, uncomfortable feeling as he flew. He had never felt uncomfortable flying, even when he was diving into the fringes of forest fires to gather coals on colliering missions. But, indeed, he could almost feel the sparks from that comet's tail. It was as if they were hot sizzling points pinging off his wings, singeing his flight feathers as the infernos of burning forests never had. He carved a great downward arc in the night to try to escape it. Was he becoming like Octavia? Could he actually feel the comet? Impossible! The comet was hundreds of thousands, millions of leagues away. Now, suddenly, those sparks were turning to glints, sparkling silvery-gray glints. "Flecks! Flecks! Flecks!" he screeched.

"Wake up, Soren! Wake up!" The huge Great Gray Owl, Twilight, was shaking him. Eglantine had flown to a perch above him and was quaking with fear at the sight of her brother writhing and screaming in his sleep. And Gylfie the Elf Owl was flying in tight little loops above him, beating the air as best she could to bring down cool drafts that might jar him from sleep and this terrible dream. Digger blinked and said, "Flecks? You mean the ones you had to pick at St. Aggie's?"

Just at that moment, Mrs. Plithiver slithered into the hollow. "Soren, dear."

"Mrs. P.," Soren gulped. He was fully awake now. "Great Glaux, did I wake you up with my screaming?"

11

"No, dear, but I just had a feeling that you were having some terrible dream. You know how we blind snakes feel things."

"Can you feel the comet, Mrs. Plithiver?"

Mrs. P. squirmed a bit then arranged herself into a neat coil. "Well, I can't really say. But it is true that since the comet arrived a lot of us nest-maid snakes have been feeling — oh, how shall I describe it — a kind of tightness in our scales. But whether it's the comet or winter coming on I don't know for sure."

Soren sighed and remembered the feeling in his dream. "Does it ever feel like hot little sparks pinging off you?"

"No, no. I wouldn't describe it that way. But, then again, I'm a snake and you're a Barn Owl."

"And why . . ." Soren hesitated. "Why is the sky bleeding?" Soren felt a shiver go through the hollow as he spoke the words.

"It's not bleeding, silly." A Spotted Owl stuck her head into the hollow. It was Otulissa. "It's merely a red tinge and it's caused by a moisture bank encountering random gases. I read all about it in Strix Miralda's book, she's a sister of the renowned weathertrix —"

"Strix Emerilla," Gylfie chimed in.

"Yes. How did you know, Gylfie?"

"Because every other word out of your mouth is a quote from Strix Emerilla."

"Well, I won't apologize. You know I think we are distantly related, although she lived centuries ago. Emerilla's sister, Miralda, was a specialist in spectography and atmospheric gases."

"Hot air," Twilight snarled. *Glaux! She frinks me off,* Twilight thought. But he did not say aloud the rather rude word for "supremely irritated."

"It's more than hot air, Twilight."

"But you aren't, Otulissa," retorted the Great Gray.

"Now, young'uns, stop your bickering," Mrs. P. said. "Soren here has had a frightfully bad dream. And I for one feel that it is not a good idea to push bad dreams away. If you feel like talking about your bad dream, Soren, please go right ahead."

But Soren really didn't feel like talking about it that much. And he had decided definitely not to tell Digger of his feelings about Octavia. His head was in too much of a muddle to be able to explain anything. There was a tense silence. But then Digger spoke up. "Soren, why 'flecks'? What made you scream out, 'flecks'?" Soren felt Gylfie give a shudder. And even Otulissa remained silent. When Soren and Gylfie had been captives at St. Aggie's they had been forced to work in the pelletorium picking apart owl pellets. Owls have a unique system for digesting their food and ridding themselves of the waste materials. All of the fur and bone and feathers of their prey are separated into small packets called pellets in their second stomach, that amazingly sensitive organ of owls, the gizzard. When all the materials were packed up, owls yarped the pellets through their beaks. In the pelletorium at St. Aggie's, they had been required to pick out the various materials like bone and feather and some mysterious element that was referred to as flecks. They never knew what flecks were exactly but they were highly prized by the brutal leaders of St. Aggie's.

"I'm not sure why. I think those sparks that come off the comet's tail somehow glinted like the flecks that we picked out of the pellets."

"Hmm," was all Digger said.

"Now look, it's almost breaklight time. Why don't you sit at my table, Soren? It'll be comfy, and I'm going to ask Matron for a nice bit of roasted vole for you."

"No can do, Mrs. P.," Otulissa said in a chipper voice.

If Mrs. P. had had eyes she would have rolled them, but instead she swung her head in an exaggerated arc and coiled up a little tighter. "What is this 'no-can-do' talk? For a supposedly educated and refined owl" — she emphasized the word refined — "I consider it a sloppy and somewhat coarse manner of speaking, Otulissa."

"There's a tropical depression that's swimming our way with the last bits of a late hurricane. The weather chaw is going out. We have to eat at the weather chaw table and . . ."

"Eat meat raw," Soren said dejectedly.

Good Glaux, raw vole on top of a bad dream and eating it literally on top of Octavia! For such were the customs of the weather and colliering chaws.

The nest-maid snakes served as tables for all the owls. They slithered into the dining halls bearing tiny Ga'Hoole nut cups of milkberry tea and whatever meat or bugs that were being served up. The chaws always ate together on the evenings of important missions. And if one was in the weather or colliering chaw, it was required that they eat their meat raw with the fur on it. Of course, Soren, like most owls until they had come to the Great Tree, had always eaten his meat raw. He still liked raw meat, but on a nippy evening like this, something warm in the gut was of great comfort. Well, he would at least try to avoid sitting next to Otulissa. Eating raw vole with that Spotted Owl yakking in his ear was enough to give any bird indigestion — or maybe even gas, and not of the random variety.

He would aim to sit between Martin and Ruby, his two best friends in the chaw. Martin was a little Northern Sawwhet, not much bigger than Gylfie, and Ruby was a Short-eared Owl.

"Glaux almighty!" Soren muttered as he approached the table of Octavia. The place between Martin and Ruby was taken by one of the new owlets who had been rescued in the Great Downing. He was a little Lesser Sooty called Silver. The name fit for he was, like all the Sooty Owls, black, but his underparts were silvery white. Sooties were all part of the same family of Barn Owls as Soren, the Tyto species, but a different group within that species — Soren being a Tyto alba and Silver a Tyto multipunctata. Still, in the whole scheme of things, they were considered "cousins." And they shared the heart-shaped face common to all Barn Owls. Silver, much smaller than Soren, now swiveled and tipped his head back.

"You shouldn't take the name of Glaux in vain, Soren." Silver spoke in a voice that was somewhere between a squeak and a shriek.

Soren blinked. "Why ever not?" Everyone said "Glaux" all the time.

"Glaux was the first Tyto. It's disrespectful to our species, to our maker."

The first Tyto, Soren thought. *What's he talking about?*

Glaux was the most ancient order of owls from which all other owls descended. Glaux was the first owl, and no one knew if it was a Tyto, let alone male or female or whatever. It didn't really matter. Apparently, Soren was not the only one confused.

"Glaux is Glaux no matter what you call him, her, whatever," said Poot. Poot was the first mate of the weather chaw but now, in the absence of Ezylryb, served as captain.

Silver blinked. "Really?"

"Yes, really," said Otulissa. "The first owl from whom we are all descended."

"I thought just Barn Owls — owls like Soren and me."

"No, *all of us*," Otulissa repeated. "No matter what kind of feather pattern, no matter what color eyes we have — yellow, amber, black, like yours — all of us are descended from Great Glaux." Otulissa could be surprising. For Otulissa to say the words "all of us" was somewhat remarkable for an owl who could be impossibly snooty and stuck-up.

It was a bit peculiar that all of the owls that had been rescued in the Great Downing had been some kind of Barn Owl. They were either Greater or Lesser Sooties like Silver, or Grass Owls, or Masked Owls. But despite the different names and slightly different coloration, they all had the distinctive heart-shaped faces that marked them as belonging to the family of Tytos, or Barn Owls. Like Silver, they had all arrived with some very strange notions and behaviors. Even the most seriously wounded owls when they were rescued had babbled nearly unintelligible fragments, but they were entranced with music. As soon as they heard Madame Plonk and the harp guild, their strange babbling had stopped.

The young owlets were getting better every day as they spent more and more time with normal owls. Of course, the owls of Ga'Hoole were not quite *normal*. When Soren was very young, his parents would tell him and Kludd and Eglantine stories. They were once-upon-a-time stories. The kind that you might wish were true but somehow don't quite believe could be. One of his and Eglantine's favorites began, "Once upon a very long time ago, in the time of Glaux, there was an order of knightly owls, from a kingdom called Ga'Hoole, who would rise each night into the blackness and perform noble deeds. They spoke no words but true ones. Their purpose was to right all wrongs, to make strong the weak, mend the broken, vanquish the proud, and make powerless those who abused the frail. With hearts sublime they would take flight . . ."

But it *was* true! And when he and Twilight and Gylfie and Digger had finally found the Great Ga'Hoole Tree on an island in the middle of the Sea of Hoolemere, Soren found that in order to fulfill this noble purpose, one needed to learn all sorts of things that many owls never learn. They learned how to read and do mathematics and, with their entry into a chaw, they learned the special skills of navigation, weather interpretation, the science of metals. This kind of learning was called the "deep knowledge" and they were taught by the "rybs." The word "ryb" itself meant deep knowledge.

Tonight, the weather chaw would fly and, for Silver and another young Masked Owl named Nut Beam, it would be their first flight with the chaw. They had not been assigned yet, or "tapped" as it was called, to the weather chaw. They were not even junior members yet. They were only going on a very minor training flight to see if possibly they might be suitable. Before his disappearance, Ezylryb seemed to be able to tell with one glance if an owl might work in the chaw. But now with him gone, Boron and Barran felt it was best for the young new owlets to be tried out for this particular chaw, which required highly refined skills.

"Are we really going to fly into a hurricane tonight?" Silver asked.

"Just a mild tropical storm," Poot answered. "Nice little depression due south of here kicking up some slop in the bight and beyond."

"When do we get to fly into a tornado?" Silver asked.

Poot blinked in disbelief. "You yoicks, young'un? You don't want to fly into a tornado. You want your wings torn off? Only owl I ever seen who got through a tornado alive with his wings came out plumb naked."

Now it was Soren's turn to blink. "Plumb naked? What do you mean?"

"Not a feather left on him. Not even a tuft of down."

Octavia gave a shiver, and their cups of milkberry tea shook. "Don't scare the young'uns, Poot."

"Look, Octavia, if they ask me I tell them."

Ruby, a deep, ruddy-colored Short-eared Owl, who was the best flier in the chaw, blinked. "How'd he fly with no feathers?"

"Not well, dearie. Not well, not well at all," Poot replied.

CHAPTER THREE
What a Blow!

Meatballs! Good and juicy." Poot swiveled his head and flung off a glob of weed, dead minnows, and assorted slop from the Sea of Hoolemere that had landed between his ear tufts.

"Storm residue. He has a very coarse way of speaking," Otulissa murmured primly to Nut Beam and Silver. She was flying between the two young owlets, and Soren was in their wake making sure that they didn't go into a bounce spiral caused by sudden updrafts, which could be dangerous.

"See? That's what you get," Poot was saying. "You don't have to go swimming to feel the water below getting warmer do you? You can feel it now, can't you?"

Soren could feel warm wet gusts coming off the waves that crashed below. It was odd, for although they were on the brink of winter, the Sea of Hoolemere in this region of the bight and beyond held the summer heat longer than any other. "That's what causes a hurricane, young'uns, when the cooler air meets up with warm water. Now, I've sent Ruby out to the edges of this mess to reconnoiter wind speeds and such."

Poot paused and looked back at his chaw members. "All right now — a little in-flight quiz."

"Oh, goody," Otulissa said. "I just love pop quizzes." Soren gave her a withering look despite the remnants of a meatball that were splattered around the rims of his eyes.

Poot continued, "Now, Martin. Which way does the wind spiral in a hurricane?"

"Oh, I know! I know!" Otulissa started waving her wings excitedly.

"Shut your beak, Otulissa," Poot snapped. "I asked Martin."

But then Nut Beam piped up, "My grandma did a special kind of dive called the spiral."

"My grandpa had a kind of twisty talon like a spiral," Silver said loudly.

"Great Glaux." Soren sighed. He had forgotten how young owlets could be. It was clear that Poot did not know how to deal with such young ones. But Otulissa interrupted what was about to turn into a free-for-all bragging match about grandparents.

"Silver, Nut Beam," she said sharply, and flew out in front of the two little owls. "Attention. All eyes on my tail, please. Now does anybody here have anything to say that is not about their grandparents, parents, or any other relatives or spirals?" There was silence. Then Silver waggled his wings. Otulissa sighed. "I feel a wing waggle from behind." She flipped her head back. "What is it, Silver?"

"My great-grandma was named for a cloud, too. Her name was Alto Cumulus."

"Thank you for that information," Otulissa said curtly. "Now may we proceed? Martin, will you please answer the question?"

"The wind spirals inward and this way." The little Northern Saw-whet spun his head almost completely around in a counterclockwise motion.

"Very good, considering you've never flown in a hurricane," Poot replied. None of them had, as yet, except for Poot.

"We might not have flown in one yet but we've read all about them, Poot," Otulissa said. "Strix Emerilla devotes three chapters to hurricanes in her book, *Atmospheric Pressures and Turbulations: An Interpreter's Guide.*"

"The most boring book in the world," Martin muttered as he flew up on Soren's starboard wing.

"I've read every word of it," Otulissa said.

"Now, next question," Poot continued. "And all you older owls shut your beaks. Which is your port wing and which is your starboard?"

There was silence. "All right. Wiggle the one you think is port." Nut Beam and Silver hesitated a bit, stole a look at each other, and then both waggled their right wing.

"Wrong!" Poot said. "Now, you two have to remember the difference. Because when I say strike off to port, or angle starboard, you're going to fly off in the wrong direction if you don't know."

Soren remembered that this was difficult for him to learn when he first started flying in the weather chaw. It took Ruby, the best flier, forever to learn port from starboard, but they all did — finally.

"All right, now," Poot said. "I'm going out for a short reconnaissance in the opposite direction of Ruby. I want to cover everything. Soren and Martin, you're in charge here. Keep flying in this direction. I'll be back soon."

Poot had not been gone long when a definite whiff seemed to wash over the small band of owls.

"I think I smell gulls nearby." Otulissa turned her beak upwind. "Oh, Great Glaux, here they come. The stench is appalling," Otulissa muttered. "Those seagulls! Scum of the avian world."

"Are they really that bad?" Nut Beam asked.

"You can smell them, can't you? And they're wet poopers on top of it all!"

"Wet poopers!" Silver and Nut Beam said at once.

"I've never met a wet pooper. I can't imagine," Nut Beam said.

"Well then, don't try," Otulissa snapped testily.

"It's hard to believe that they never yarp pellets at all," Nut Beam continued to muse.

"My sister actually had a friend who was a wet pooper, but they wouldn't let her bring him home. I think he was a warbler," Silver announced.

"Oh, Glaux, here we go again," said Martin.

"I think maybe I've met one once," said Nut Beam.

"Well, it's not something to be proud of. It's disgusting," Otulissa replied.

"You're starting to sound like a nest-maid snake, Otulissa," said Soren, and laughed. Nest-maid snakes were notoriously disdainful of all birds except owls because of what they considered their inferior and less noble digestive systems due to their inability to yarp pellets. All of their waste was splatted out from the other end, which nest-maids considered vile and disgusting.

"They give us a lot of good information about weather, Otulissa," Soren said.

"You mean a lot of dirty jokes. You can find good information in books."

Poot was soon back with the seagulls in his wake.

"What's the report?" Martin asked.

"Storm surge moderate," Poot said, "but building. The gulls say the leading edge of this thing is at least fifty leagues off to the southeast."

"Yeah, but I got news for you." At that moment, Ruby skidded in on a tumultuous draft and a mess of flying spume. She was accompanied by two gulls. It was as if she had come out of nowhere. And suddenly Soren felt an immense pull on his downwind wings. "You've been talking to the wrong gulls. It's not just a storm with a leading edge. It's a hurricane with an eye!"

Hurricane! Soren thought. *Impossible. How has this happened so quickly?* No one except Poot had ever flown a hurricane — and these young owlets! What ever would happen to them?

"It's still far off," Ruby continued. "But it's moving faster than you think and building stronger. And we're very near a rain band. And then it's the eye wall!"

"Eye wall! We've got to alter course," Poot exclaimed. "Which way, Ruby?"

"Port, I mean starboard!"

"The eye wall!" Soren and Martin both gasped. The eye wall of a hurricane was worse than the eye. It was a wall of thunderstorms that was preceded by the rain bands that delivered violent swirling updrafts that could extend hundreds of leagues from this wall.

"You can't see the band from here because of the clouds."

Oh, Glaux, thought Soren. *Don't let these young owlets go off on their stories of grandparents being named for clouds.*

"I think that right now we might actually be between two rain bands," Ruby continued.

And then it was as if they all were sucked up into a swirling shaft. *This IS a hurricane!* Soren thought. He saw Martin go spinning by in a tawny blur. "Martin!" he screamed. He heard a sickening gasp and in the blur saw the little beak of the Saw-whet open in a wheeze as Martin tried to gulp air. He must have been in one of the terrible airless vacuums that Soren had heard about. Then Martin vanished, and Soren had to fight with all of his might to stay back up, belly down, and flying. He could not believe how difficult this was. He had flown through blazing forests harvesting live coals, battling the enormous fire winds and strange contortions of air that the heat made, but this was terrible!

"Strike off to port, south by southeast. We're going to run down. Rudder starboard with tail feathers! Extend lulus." The lulus were small feathers just at the bend of an owl's wing, which could help smooth the airflow. Poot was now calling out a string of instructions. "Downwind rudder, hold two points to skyward with port wing. Come on, chaw! You can do it! Primary feathers screw down. Level off now. Forward thrust!" Poot was flying magnificently, especially considering that under the lee of his wings he had tucked the two young owlets Nut Beam and Silver for protection.

But where was Martin? Martin was the smallest owl in the chaw. *Concentrate! Concentrate!* Soren told himself. *You're a dead bird if you think about anything but flying. Dead bird! Dead bird! Wings torn off!* All the horrible stories he had heard about hurricanes came back to Soren. And although owls talked about the deadly eye of the hurricane, he knew there was something worse, really — the rim of that eye. And if the eye was fifty leagues away — well, the rim could be much closer. Soren's own two eyes opened wide in terror and his third eyelid, the transparent one that swept across this eyeball, had to work hard to clear the debris, the slop, being flung in it from all directions. But he paid no heed to the slop. In his eye was the image of little Martin vanishing in a split second and being sucked directly into that rim. The eye of a hurricane was calm, but caught in the rim, a bird could spin around and around, its wings torn off by the second spin and most likely gasping for air until it died.

The air started to smooth out and the clammy warmth that had welled up from below subsided as a cooler layer of air floated up from the turbulent waters. But it had begun to pour hard. A driving rain pushed by the winds slanted in at a steep angle. The sea below seemed to smoke from the force of the rain.

"Form up, chaw! SOFP," Poot commanded. They all assumed the positions of their Standard Operational Flight Pattern. Soren swiveled his head to look for Martin off his starboard wing. There was a little blank space where the Northern Saw-whet usually flew. He tipped his head up to where Ruby flew and saw the rusty fluff of her underbelly. She looked down and shook her head sadly. Soren thought he saw a tear well up in her eye, but it could have been some juice from a leftover meatball.

"Roll call!" Poot now barked. "Beak off, chaw!"

"Ruby here!" snapped the rust-colored Short-eared Owl.

"Otulissa here!"

"Soren here!"

Then there was nothing — silence, or perhaps it was more like a small gulp from the position that Martin had always flown.

"Absence noted. Continue," Poot said.

Absence noted? Continue? Was that it? Soren gasped. But before he could protest there was that piercing little voice, "Silver here."

"Nut Beam here! But I'm feeling nauseous."

"WHERE IS MARTIN, FOR GLAUX'S SAKE!" Soren shrieked in rage.

"Owl down," Poot said, "Search-and-rescue commence."

Then there was a muffled, slightly gagging sound and a terrific stench. At first, Soren thought Nut Beam had thrown up. But then out of the smoking Sea of Hoolemere, a seagull rose and in its beak was a wet little form.

"Martin here!" gasped the little owl. He hung limply in the beak of the seagull.

CHAPTER FOUR
The Spirit Woods

I'm not sure if it was the impact on the water or the stench that got me, but I'm still feeling a bit dizzy. I have to say, however, that seagull stench is now my favorite fragrance." Martin turned and nodded at Smatt, the seagull who had rescued him.

"Aw, it warn't nothin.'" The seagull ducked his head modestly.

When he had first vanished, Martin had been sucked straight up, but it was a narrow funnel of warm air and almost immediately it had swirled into a bank of cold air that created a downdraft, and Martin had plunged into the sea. Smatt, who had been navigating between these funnels of warm and cold air, plunged in after him and grabbed him in his beak as he might have grabbed a fish — although Martin was considerably smaller than any fish that seagulls normally ate.

They had lighted down now on the mainland, in a wooded area on a peninsula that fingered out into the sea.

It seemed, for the moment, calm. Although Soren, as he glanced around, found the forest quite strange. All the trees were white-barked and not one had a single leaf. Indeed, although it was night, this forest had a kind of luminance that made the moon pale by comparison.

"I would guess," said Otulissa as she studied the sky, "that we are between rain bands here." For some reason this rankled Soren. It sounded to him as if Otulissa was trying to sum up the weather situation the way Ezylryb would have, being the most knowledgeable owl of all about weather. Poot, who had succeeded him as chaw captain, really had very little knowledge in comparison, but he was a great flier. Now it seemed as if Otulissa had become the self-appointed weather expert.

Poot looked around uneasily. "That, or a spirit woods."

A chill ran through them all. "A spirit woods?" Martin said softly. "I've heard of them."

"Yeah, you've heard of them. You don't necessarily want to spend the night in them," Poot replied.

"I don't know, Poot," Ruby spoke in a nervous low voice, "whether we've got much choice. I mean that hurricane's still going. I've seen the worst of it. It's not something you want to mess with."

"Well, folks." Smatt began to lift his wings. A fetid smell wafted toward them. "I think I'll be clearing out now." The seagull looked apprehensively at Poot. In a flash he had lifted off and vanished.

"What are we gonna do, Poot?" Silver asked, a slight tremor in his voice.

"Not much choice, as Ruby said. Just hope we don't disturb any scrooms."

"Scrooms!" Nut Beam and Silver wailed.

"Well, I don't believe in them," Martin said and stomped his small talons into the moss-covered ground. Then, as if to prove it, he lifted off and began to search for a tree to light down in.

"You mind what tree you choose. You don't want to disturb a scroom," Poot called after him. But Soren thought that maybe after having been sucked up in a rain band, then dropped into the sea, a scroom was nothing to Martin.

Scrooms were disembodied spirits of owls who had died and had not quite made it all the way to glaumora, which was the special owl heaven where the souls of owls went. Nut Beam and Silver, however, had begun to cry uncontrollably.

"Pull yourselves together, both of you," Otulissa exploded angrily. "There's no such thing as scrooms. An atmospheric disturbance. False light. That's all. Strix Emerilla has written about it in a very erudite book entitled, *Spectroscopic Anomalies: Shifts in Shape and Light.*"

"Yes, there are scrooms!" the two owlets hooted back shrilly.

"My grandma said so," Nut Beam said defiantly and stomped a small talon on the moss.

"I've heard enough about your grandmas," Otulissa snapped. "Poot, how long do we have to stay here?"

"Until the hurricane blows through. Can't take these young'uns" — he nodded toward Silver and Nut Beam — "out in this. Too inexperienced."

"You're making us stay here — with scrooms?" Nut Beam protested. And as if on cue, Silver started to wail again.

Ruby flew up and then lighted directly in front of the two owlets. She looked almost twice her size as her rust-colored feathers had puffed up in the manner of owls who are extremely angry. In the pale eerie white of the forest, Ruby looked like a ball of red-hot embers. "I'm fed up with all your whining. I don't give a pile of racdrops if there're scrooms here. I'm hungry. I'm tired. I want a nice fat rat or vole. I'll take squirrel if I have to. Then I want to go to sleep. And you two better shut your beaks because I'll make your life more miserable than scrooms ever could!" The other owls looked at Ruby with astonishment.

"I think we need to organize a hunting party," Otulissa said.

"Yes, yes, immediately," Poot said. He began to flutter about the group. "Now, there's no telling what one can find in such a woods."

It was obvious to Soren, Ruby, and Martin that Otulissa had embarrassed Poot, who might be a terrific flier but not a natural leader. They felt the absence of Ezylryb more than ever.

But then, Poot seemed to be jarred into action. He swelled up with authority and tried his best to sound like a leader. "Soren," Poot said, "you and Ruby can cover the northeast quadrant of this woods. You fly it hard now, young'uns. We got some hungry beaks here. Martin and Otulissa can cover the southwest one. I'll stay here with the young'uns."

"Ha!" Ruby gave a harsh sound and ascended through the branches. "I think Poot's scared of scrooms. That's why he sent us out. You scared, Soren?" They had gained some altitude now, and the strange mist that floated through the white trees below seemed to evaporate.

"Sort of," Soren said.

"Well, at least you're honest. But what do you mean by 'sort of'?"

"I think the idea of a scroom is not so much scary as sad. I mean scrooms are supposed to be spirits that didn't quite make it to glaumora. That's kind of sad."

"I guess so," Ruby said.

Guess so? Soren blinked at Ruby. He thought it was terribly sad, but Ruby wasn't the deepest owl. She was a fantastic flier and a great chaw mate and lots of fun but, although she felt things in her gizzard like all owls, she was not given to reflecting deeply. But now she surprised him. "How come they don't make it to glaumora?"

"I'm not sure. Mrs. P. said that it was because they might have unfinished business on earth."

"Mrs. Plithiver? How would she know? She's a snake."

"I sometimes think that Mrs. P. knows more about owls than owls do." Soren cocked his head suddenly. "Sssh." Ruby shut her beak immediately. She, like all other owls, had great respect for the extraordinary hearing abilities of Barn Owls. "Ground squirrel below."

There were actually three in all. And Ruby, who was incredibly fast with her talons, managed to get two in one single slicing swipe. They were more successful than Martin and Otulissa, who had only come back with two very small mice.

"Hunter's share," Poot said, nodding to the four of them. It was customary that the owls who did the hunting got first choice of the catch. Soren chose a thigh from his ground squirrel. It was rather scrawny, and it wasn't the most flavorful ground squirrel he had ever eaten. Maybe a spirit wood wasn't the best place for a ground squirrel to get plump and juicy. Then Soren had a creepy thought. Maybe they fed on scrooms or perhaps scrooms fed on them — spirit food. His gizzard hardly had to work to pack in those bones and fur.

By the time they had finished eating, the night was thinning into day. Although with the mist that seemed to wrap itself through the branches of the white-barked trees, Soren thought that it seemed like twilight in these woods.

"I think," Poot announced, "it's time for us to turn in. Not for a full day's sleep, mind you. We'll leave before First Black. No fear of crows around here." He slid his neck about in a slow twist as if scanning the wood.

"No. Just scrooms," Nut Beam said.

"Nut Beam, shut your beak," Martin screeched fiercely.

"Now, now, Martin! Don't like that tone, lad," Poot said, trying to sound very —

Very what? wondered Soren. *Like Ezylryb? Never like the Captain.*

"Well, I've been doing some thinking," Poot went on to say. "And I think that this being a spirit woods as some calls 'em, I think it's best that we keep to the ground for sleeping, no perching in them trees." He swiveled his head around in a slow sweeping movement, as if he were almost trying to push back the bone-white trees that surrounded them.

A hush fell upon the group. Soren thought he could hear the beat of their hearts quicken. *This scroom stuff must really be serious,* he said to himself. Even Ruby looked a little nervous. For an owl to sleep on the ground was almost unheard of, unless, of course, it was a Burrowing Owl who lived in the desert, like Digger. There were dangers on the ground. Predators — like raccoons.

"I know what you be thinking," Poot continued nervously and seemed to avoid looking them in the eye as Ezylryb would have. "I know you're thinking that for an owl to ground sleep ain't natural. But these ain't natural woods. And it's said that these trees might really belong to the scrooms. You never know which one a scroom might light down in and it's best to leave the trees be. I'm older than you young'uns. Got more experience. And I'd be daft not to tell you that my gizzard is giving me some mighty twinges."

"Mine, too!" said Silver.

"Probably has a gizzard the size of a pea," Martin whispered.

"Now don'cha go worry too much. We just got to be vigi-ful," Poot continued.

"You mean 'vigilant'?" Otulissa said.

"Don't smart beak me, lassie. We's gonna set up a

watch. I'll take the first one with Martin. Otulissa and Ruby you take the next. And Soren you take the last. You have to do it alone, but it be the shortest one, lad. So nothin' to fear."

Nothing to fear? Then why doesn't he take it? Soren thought, but he knew that the one thing a chaw owl never did was question a command. All of the owls turned their heads toward Soren.

Martin stepped forward. "I'll stay up with you, Soren."

Soren blinked at the little Northern Saw-whet. "No, no — that's very kind of you, Martin, but you'll be tired. You must already be tired. I mean you've fallen into the sea. Don't worry, Martin. I'll be fine."

"No, Soren, I mean it."

"No, I'll be fine," Soren said firmly.

The truth was that during that first watch they were all too nervous to sleep and the ground was a terrible place to even try to sleep to begin with. But as the dark faded and the white of the trees melted into the lightness of the morning, they did grow sleepier and sleepier. The owls' heads began to droop lower and lower until they were resting on their breasts or on their backs, as it was the habit of very young owls to twist their heads around and rest them just between their shoulders.

"Your watch, Soren," Ruby said.

His eyes blinked open. He lifted his head.

"Don't worry. There is nothing out here. Not a raccoon, not a scroom, not a scroom of a raccoon." Otulissa churred softly, which was the sound that owls made when they laughed.

Soren walked over to the watch mound that was in a small clearing. He spread his wings and, in one brief upstroke, rose to settle on the top of the mound. The fog in the forest had thickened again. A soft breeze swirled through the woods, stirring and spinning the mist into fluffy shapes. Some of the mist clouds were long and skinny, others puffy. Soren thought of the silly jabber of the young owlets when they had been flying earlier, before encountering the hurricane. The owlets were sort of cute, he guessed, in their own annoying little way. It was hard to believe, however, that he had ever been that young. He had barely known his parents before he had been snatched, and he had never known his grandparents. There had been no time. He blinked his eyes at the mist that was now whirling into new shapes. It was strange how one could start to read this ground mist like clouds, find pictures in them — a raccoon, a deer bounding over a tree stump, a fish leaping from a river. Soren had tried sometimes to make up stories about cloud pictures when he was flying. The vapors just ahead of him had clumped together into one large shapeless mass, but now they seemed to be pulling apart again into two clumps. There was something vaguely familiar about the shapes that these clumps were becoming. What was it? A lovely downy bundle that looked so soft and warm. Something seemed to call to him and yet there was no sound. How could that be?

Soren grew very still. Something was happening. He was not frightened. No, not frightened at all. But sad, yes, deeply and terribly sad. He felt himself drawn to these two shapes. They were fluffy and their heads were cocked in such a familiar way as if they were listening to him. And they *were* calling to him, and they were saying things but there were no sounds. It was as if the voices were sealed inside his head. Just then, he felt himself step out of his body. He felt his wings spread. He was lifting, and yet he was still there on the mound. He could see his talons planted on the mossy top with the tangle of ivy. But, at the same time, he could see something moving out of him. It was him — but not him. It was his shape, pale and misty and swirling like the other shapes. The thing that was him but not him was lifting, rising, and spreading its wings in flight to perch in the big white tree at the edge of the clearing where the two other misty figures perched.

False light?

No, not false light, Soren.

Scrooms?

If you must.

Mum? Da?

The mist seemed to shiver and glint like moonlight scattered on water.

He floated over the mound but when he looked back he saw his own figure still standing there. He extended a talon but it was transparent! And then he lighted down on the branch. In that instant, Soren realized he felt in a strange way complete. It was as if there had been a hole in his gizzard and now it had been filled and closed. He reached out with his talon to touch his mum but it simply passed through her.

Am I dying? Am I becoming a scroom?

No, dearest. No one had called him "dearest" like that since he had been snatched.

Soren cocked his head and tried to look at his parents, but the mist was continually shifting, sliding, and recomposing itself into their shapes. They were recognizable but yet it was not images he was seeing. It was more like a foggy shadow. Still, he knew without a doubt it was them.

But why, why after all this time were they here, seeking him out?

Unfinished business? Is that what it is?

We think so. It was the voice of his father in his head.

You don't know?

Not exactly, dear. We're never sure. We know something isn't right. We have feelings, but no real answers to these feelings.

Are you trying to warn me of something?

Yes, yes. But the hard part is we don't know what it is we should warn you about.

Soren wondered if they knew about Kludd. He wanted to tell them how Kludd had pushed him from the nest, but he couldn't. Something stopped in his brain. Words began to tumble out of his mouth, and now he could actually hear those words. He was telling them about Kludd, but his mum and da were unmoved. They were not hearing anything of what he was saying. And there was a blankness now in his head. This was all very weird. When he could hear his own voice, the words in the normal way, his parents could not. Their only way of speaking to one another was this silent language that seemed to exist only in their heads. And yet Soren could not form the ideas in his head to tell them about Kludd, and they could not tell him about the danger.

Metal! Beware Metal Beak! The words exploded in

Soren's head. It was the voice of his father but it seemed to have taken all his energy to do this. His father was dissolving before his eyes. His mother as well. The mists that had been their shapes were swirling, seeping away. Soren reached out with his talons to hold them. "Don't go! Don't go. Don't leave me! Come back."

"What's you yelling about, lad? Wake us all up, will you?" Soren was suddenly on the ground, and Poot was standing in front of him, blinking. How had he gotten on the ground? He had been in that tree a second ago but he had no memory of flying down from it. And there was no mist now. None at all.

"I'm sorry, Poot. I flew up into that tree there. I thought I saw something." Soren nodded.

"No, you didn't," Poot said. "I woke a few minutes ago. You were standing right here on the mound. Perfectly alert — being a good lookout. Believe me, I would have had your tail feathers if you hadn't been."

"I was right here?" Soren was incredulous.

"Course you were, young'un," Poot said and looked at him curiously as if he'd gone yoicks. "Right here you were. I would have noticed you up in the tree, believe me."

Had it just been a dream? Soren thought. *But it felt so real. I heard Mum's and Da's voices in my head. It* was *real.*

"Time we be takin' off." Poot looked at the sky that was

turning a dusky purple. Pink clouds sliding against it. "Wind's going our way," Poot remarked, after studying the clouds for a minute. "We'll catch a westerly and come in on a nice reach." A reach was easy flying with the wind being not on the beak or on the tail feathers directly, but a little aft of the wing, giving a nice steady boost to their flight. The others were beginning to stir from their daytime slumbers.

"Form up!" Poot commanded. It was to be a ground start, which was a bit harder than taking off from a branch. But they did it nonetheless. Soren and Martin were the last to rise in flight. They ascended in tight spiraling circles and were soon clear of the spirit woods.

When Soren looked back, he saw the mist gathering again. Like silky scarves, it began to wind through the trees. He strained his eyes to find those two familiar shapes. Just one more glimpse, that's all he wanted. One more glimpse. But the mist lay thick and shapeless over the white forest. Had Soren been able to see through it, however, he might have spotted a feather, just like one of his, but nearly transparent, drifting lazily down from the branch of a tree in the spirit woods.

CHAPTER FIVE
Bubo's Forge

Soren had been back for two days. But he had said nothing of his strange experience in the spirit woods to anyone, not even his closest friends, his friends in the "band" — Gylfie, Digger, Twilight, himself, and now, since her rescue, his sister, Eglantine. But every day when he fell to sleep he dreamed of the scrooms of his parents. Had it been a dream in the spirit woods as well, just a dream? And the words *Metal Beak*, those two words seemed to almost clang in his brain and send ominous quivers to his gizzard. The words took on a life of their own and grew more dreadful with each passing hour.

"Something's spooking you, Soren, I just know it," Digger said as they were sitting in the library one evening after navigation practice.

"No, nothing at all," Soren said quickly. Soren had been reading a really good book, but he was distracted and had read the same sentence about five times. Leave it to Digger to pick up on the worries that haunted him day and night.

"Nothing at all, Soren?" Digger blinked and looked at him closely. The fluffy white brow tufts that framed his deep yellow eyes waggled a bit.

Soren looked back at Digger. *Should I tell him about the scrooms—about Metal Beak? The best thing is to be honest, yet ...*

"Digger, something is bothering me, but I can't tell you just now. Do you understand?"

Digger blinked again. "Of course, Soren. When you're ready to tell, I'll listen," the Burrowing Owl said softly. "No need to say anything until you're ready."

"Thank you, Digger, thank you so much."

So the Barn Owl got up, closed the book he was reading, and went to put it on the shelf. The shelf was next to the table where Ezylryb always sat absorbed in his studies, munching on his little pile of dried caterpillars. The library wasn't the same without the old Screech Owl. Nothing seemed the same without him. Soren slid the book back into its place on the shelf. As he turned to leave, a book on metals caught his eye. Metals! Why hadn't he thought of this before? He must go to see Bubo, the blacksmith. He must immediately go to Bubo's forge. Soren might not be ready to tell Digger, but he was ready to tell Bubo — not all of it, but part of it — the part about Metal Beak.

He flew out of the Great Ga'Hoole Tree, spiraled down

toward its base, and then swept low across the ground to a nearby cave. This was Bubo's forge. The forge was just outside the entry of the cave and the rock had blackened over the years from Bubo's fires. It was to this forge that Soren and the other members of the colliering chaw brought the live coals that fed the fires, which smelted the metals used for everything from pots and pans to battle claws and shields for the great tree. If anyone knew about metal beaks, or whatever it was that the scrooms had spoken of in the whispery voices that still swirled in Soren's head, it would be Bubo. The fire had been dampened down, however, and there was no sign of Bubo. Perhaps he was inside.

Although Bubo was not a Burrowing Owl, who always made their nests in the ground, he preferred living in a cave to a tree. As he had once explained to Soren, blacksmiths like himself, no matter if they were Great Horned Owls, Snowies, Spotted, or Great Grays, were drawn to the earth where, indeed, the metals lodged.

Soren now stepped into the shadow of the overhanging rock ledge of the cave's opening. Deep inside, he could see the glints of the whirlyglasses that Bubo had strung up. These contraptions were made from bits of colored glass and when light crept into the cave and struck the glass, reflections spun through the air and bounced off the walls in swirling dapples of color. There was no moonlight tonight, though. It was the time of the dwenking when the moon disappeared to barely a sliver.

"Bubo!" Soren called. He waited. "Bubo!"

"That you, Soren?" A large shadowy bundle of feathers started to melt out of the darkness of the cave. Great Horned Owls like Bubo were large, but Bubo himself was unusually large and towered over Soren. His two ear tufts, which grew straight up over each eye, were exceedingly bushy, giving him a slightly threatening demeanor. But Soren knew that beneath the gruffness there was no owl who had a gentler heart than Bubo. Although, like most Great Horned Owls, his feathers were basically the dull somber grays, browns, and blacks, they had been shot through with bright red and hot yellow like the hottest of fires — the ones said to have "bonk." Bonk was the word that blacksmiths like Bubo used to describe the strongest and most energetic fires. Such fires have special hues and colors unlike ordinary ones. Bubo also could be said to have bonking colorful plumage. It was as if he had been clothed in the flames of his own forge instead of just the usual drab feathers of his species. "What brings you here, lad?"

"Metal Beak," Soren blurted without preamble.

"Metal Beak!" Bubo gasped. "What'cha know about him, laddie?"

"Him?" Soren blinked. "It's a him?" Until that moment, Soren thought that the scrooms of his parents had been referring to a thing — something that struck dread in him, like flecks. Yes, he had suspected flecks because it was Bubo himself who had first explained to him that the flecks they had been forced to pick at St. Aggie's were a kind of special metal with what he had called "magnetic properties." He had said that when all the tiny unseeable parts, the flecks in these metals were lined up, it created a force that was called magnetic. Now Soren didn't know what to think. He was relieved that Metal Beak had nothing to do with flecks. But why was Bubo so agitated? The big, flaming Horned Owl was almost hopping out of his feathers.

"You stay clear of him. You ain't to go tangling with that owl, Soren."

"Metal Beak is an owl?"

"Oh, yeah."

"What kind?"

"No one is for sure what kind he be. A bad kind, that's all I can tell you."

Soren was confused. "How can you not be sure about what kind he is?"

"Because he wears a metal beak and a metal mask over most his face."

"Why's that?"

"Wouldn't really know," Bubo said as if he didn't really want to discuss it. "Some say he flies noisy like a Pygmy Owl, but he ain't no pygmy size, I'll tell you that. Well, maybe Barn Owl but bigger, much bigger, but not as big as a Great Gray. Some swear he's got ear tufts like a Great Horned, yours truly here. Others say no. But there's one thing they all agree on."

"What's that?"

Bubo's voice dropped. "He's the most brutal owl in all the kingdoms of owls. He's the most vicious owl on earth."

Soren swore that he felt his gizzard drop to his talons. When Soren and his band had been on their journey to the Great Ga'Hoole Tree, they had come across a dying Barred Owl. To Soren and his mates it looked like a murder by St. Aggie's top lieutenants.

"Was it St. Aggie's?" Glyfie had asked. And the dying Barred Owl had responded with his last breath. "I wish it had been St. Aggie's. It was something far worse. Believe me — St. Aggie's — Oh! You only wish!"

Soren, Gylfie, Twilight, and Digger could not imagine anything worse, anything more brutal than St. Aggie's. But the Barred Owl had told them differently. There *was* something far worse. It was nameless and now possibly faceless, but so frightened were the four owls that they had begun to refer to this monster or possibly monsters as the "you only wish." The few times they had begun to ask about this evil thing, the owls of the Ga'Hoole Tree, the rybs, had deftly turned the conversation to something else. But now Bubo was telling him of this brutal owl known as Metal Beak.

Bubo would never turn away from a young owl's question. That simply wasn't his style. So Soren did not feel reluctant to press him. "You know, Bubo, how Gylfie, Digger, Twilight, and I found that dying Barred Owl in The Beaks?"

"Yes, I heard tell of that and the bobcat that you four young'uns managed to kill right stylishly, I'd say. Dropped a coal in his eye, direct hit from how far up was it?"

"Oh, I'm not sure, Bubo. But tell me this — do you think that the Barred Owl might have been done in by this Metal Beak?"

"Very possible! Possible, indeed. Maybe even probable, which, as you know if you study your arithmetic, can happen more often than possible. In other words, probable is more possible than possible."

"Yes, yes, of course." Bubo could go off in this way, and it could be very difficult to get him back on track. "I see what you mean. But why would it be very possible, or maybe even probable, that this Metal Beak killed the Barred Owl?"

"Well, the Barred Owl were a rogue smith, warn't he." But it really wasn't a question. Soren wasn't quite sure if he understood Bubo's meaning. It was as if Bubo was saying that if an owl was a rogue smith, this sometimes could happen.

"Yes," said Soren hesitantly. "But . . ."

"But what?"

"Well, Bubo, I am not sure exactly what a rogue smith is."

"Don't know what a rogue smith is, don't you?"

Soren shook his head and looked down at his talons.

"Nothing to be ashamed about, lad. A rogue smith is a blacksmith just like me. But he ain't attached to any kingdom. I mean, we here at the Ga'Hoole Tree be the only ones who know how to use fire in all different ways, like for cooking, and the light for the candles for reading and, of course, for tools, like battle claws, and pots and pans and cauldrons. But these rogue smiths, they know about forging some and they mostly make battle claws. Weapons, you know."

"But who do they make them for?"

"Anyone who comes along. They don't ask no questions about the who, but seems like they get plenty of information one way or the other. They have to deal with rogue colliers. Get a lot from them."

"Rogue colliers? You mean colliers like me and Otulissa and Martin and Ruby?"

"Yep, but no chaw. You get it? They just go it alone."

"Alone into forest fires?"

Bubo nodded. "But it's the smiths who really get all the good information. This Barred was a slipgizzle."

"Yes," Soren replied.

"Now, you know what a slipgizzle is, don't you?"

"Uh . . . kind of a secret agent owl?"

"That's it, basically. Keeps their eyes and ears open for any news, then reports back to us. But they never stay long when they come. They likes living wild. I think I recall this Barred Owl coming in here once a while back. A rough-trade sort of bird. Didn't like his meat cooked, no sirree. Said candlelight, smell of wax wobbled his gizzard."

"Are there any other rogue smiths?" Soren asked. An idea was forming in his head.

"Oh, yes — a few. There's a Snowy Owl over near the border between The Barrens and Silverveil."

"Do you know his name?" Soren asked.

"His? What makes you think it's a 'his'?"

"Hers?" Soren asked tentatively. Bubo nodded. "I've never heard of a female blacksmith."

"Well, now you have." Bubo batted his talon on one of the whirlyglasses and the colors seemed to ignite as they were caught in the light of a candle dappling the walls of the cave.

"What's her name?" Soren asked.

"Don't know. Most of them rogue smiths keep their names to themselves. They're an odd sort, I'm telling you." Then he looked narrowly at Soren and fixed him in his amber gaze. "Rogues are unpredictable and not only that, they are often visited by bad sorts. After all, they make weapons. So, Soren, don't you be getting ideas."

But that was just exactly what Soren was doing: getting an idea!

CHAPTER SIX
Eglantine's Dilemma

B eware of Metal Beak.' It was the scrooms who told me." Soren was in the hollow with Twilight, Gylfie, Digger, and Eglantine.

"But did they actually say it out loud?" Gylfie hopped up close to Soren and looked straight up.

"Well, no — not exactly. Scrooms don't speak out loud."

"Then how do you know," Eglantine asked in a broken voice, "that it was them, the scrooms of Mum and Da? Because if it was, that means they are dead, doesn't it, Soren?" Tears began to leak out of his sister's coal-black eyes.

"It does, Eglantine, and there is nothing we can do about that," said Soren.

"Dead is dead," Twilight said in his usual blunt way. Gylfie turned and kicked him in his talons.

"What did you do that for, Gylfie?"

"Twilight, she has just found out for sure that her parents are dead. You could be a little more sensitive!"

"But it's the truth, isn't it?" Twilight said, slightly abashed by Gylfie's reprimand.

"It is, and it isn't," Soren said. "You asked me how I heard them, how I could be sure. I can't explain exactly. It was them. I felt their spirits, and their words were not out-loud words but seemed to form in my brain. First, they would come like fog or mist, and then they would gather into a shape that had meaning, a picture. But I felt so close to them. I knew it was them."

Digger now spoke. "But why do you say that it is and it isn't true that they are dead, Soren?"

"Mrs. Plithiver told me that one reason the scrooms of owls do not go to glaumora is because they have unfinished business on earth. I think Mum and Da's unfinished business was to warn me about Metal Beak. We must find this Metal Beak, and I think that the best way is to go to the rogue smith of Silverveil."

"But we can't, Soren," Eglantine said in an almost whiny voice. "I have navigation and Ga'Hoolology, and they really get mad at us new owls if we skip class. Especially the Ga'Hoolology ryb. She says that these are the most important days for the tree."

Ga'Hoolology was the study and care of the great tree, which not only gave habitat to the owls of Ga'Hoole but nourishment through its nuts and berries. Indeed, there was hardly a part of the tree that was not used in some way.

"Yes, but the berry harvest is coming up," Soren said.

"So?" said Eglantine.

"It's a big festival." Gylfie turned to Eglantine. "There are no chaw practices or classes for three days. We all have to help with the harvest and then on the third night, there's a big banquet that goes on every night for another three or four at least, to celebrate. They say the rybs always get very tipsy on the milkberry wine. It'll be the easiest time to fly off with no one noticing."

"Oh," said Eglantine. She sounded slightly deflated as if some last hope had vanished for her. "So when does this festival start?"

"Five days," Digger said.

"Five days!" Eglantine sounded panicked.

"Yes," said Soren. "But we shouldn't plan to leave until after the banquet is really going. The banquets don't begin for another eight days."

"Yes, yes," everyone agreed. They began making plans immediately. Should it just be the five of them or should they include others like Martin and Ruby? Soren felt it might be a good idea because colliers knew the ways of smiths and other colliers and, quite honestly, Soren realized he did not want to take on the entire burden with this rogue smith. She might prove difficult. He wondered to himself if Eglantine was really strong enough to go yet. She still seemed frail to him — even though it had been almost two months since her rescue — not just physically frail, but frail in the gizzard. Then again, would her feelings be hurt if she were left behind?

"What about Otulissa?" Gylfie asked.

There was a resounding "No!"

"She can't keep her beak shut," said Twilight.

"Right," said Digger. "She'll be hooting about it all over the tree."

"I can come, can't I, Soren?" Eglantine asked in a small tremulous voice.

"Do you feel strong enough?"

"Of course I do!"

Soren didn't have the heart to say no.

Then another thought suddenly occurred to him. "You know, all this time I have been thinking that this Metal Beak, whoever he is, might be the one who killed the Barred Owl. Do you suppose that —"

It was as if the three owls, Twilight, Digger, and Gylfie, all read Soren's mind. "Ezylryb," they all gasped.

"Exactly. Do you think Metal Beak could have something to do with Ezylryb's disappearance?" The owls began whispering in excited voices.

"We must work out our strategy," Gylfie said.

"We better go to the library and look at maps of Silver-veil," Digger added.

"Well, Bubo said the rogue smith was on the border between Silverveil and The Barrens. So doesn't that mean it could be in either place?" Soren asked.

"But they call her the rogue smith of Silverveil," Gylfie said. "So most likely she is closer to Silverveil."

There were countless details to work out. Should they "borrow" battle claws from the armory? No, they would be found out immediately even if the older owls were tipsy. Could they leave any earlier? What weather was coming in? If it was a south wind and they were flying south by southeast, it could slow them down. Amid all this jabber there was one little pocket of silence. And that was when Eglantine retreated to her own corner of the hollow and tried to weep as silently as possible in the fluffy nest of down. But it wasn't her mum's down. It didn't smell anything like her mum, and there was too much moss in it. But she couldn't let Soren see her crying. She had just told him that she was strong enough to fly with them to Silverveil. She wanted to be included so much. They mustn't think she was a baby. Well, there was only one place to go when she was feeling this bad — to Mrs. Plithiver. She hoped Mrs. P.'s hollow mates — two other nest-maid snakes — wouldn't be there. It would be all over the tree if they saw her crying. Nest-maids were notorious gossips.

"There, there, dear." Mrs. Plithiver had coiled up and was stretching as far as possible to stroke Eglantine's wing. "It can't be that bad."

"But it is, Mrs. P. You don't understand."

"No, I don't. Why don't you start at the beginning?"

So Eglantine told the old nest-maid snake about what Soren had seen in the spirit forest, about the scrooms of their parents, and how Twilight had said "dead is dead." But Soren had said "not exactly" and the part about Metal Beak and the unfinished business. "See, Mrs. P., I know this is wrong but if the business gets finished, Mum and Da will go to glaumora, and then I'll never see them again."

Mrs. Plithiver was silent for a long time. If she had had eyes they might have wept. Finally, she spoke. "It's not wrong, Eglantine, to want to see your parents again, but the real question is would you be happy if you saw them — or their scrooms — and they were very, very sad and worried about you?"

Eglantine blinked. She hadn't thought of that.

"Was Soren happy?" Mrs. P. continued. "Did he say anything about being so happy and glad to have seen them?"

Now that Eglantine thought about it, Soren hadn't seemed at all happy since he had returned from the spirit woods. He seemed completely dragged down by something. And Mrs. Plithiver, as if seeing directly into Eglantine's brain, said, "It's the scrooms. Scrooms with unfinished business, although they seem only to be made of mist and vapor, can be a terrible weight on the living. I noticed it as soon as Soren returned."

"You did?" Eglantine blinked in astonishment. Mrs. P. nodded her rose-colored head, and her eye dents seemed to flinch. "How?" Eglantine asked.

"I've told you, Eglantine, that although we are blind, nest-maid snakes have very finely tuned sensibilities. We pick up on these things, especially if it concerns family members, and I worked for your family for so long — well, I just know when any one of you is out of sorts. But, Eglantine, the main thing is that you must rid yourself of this notion that to see your parents just one more time, to meet their scrooms, would make you feel happy. It won't, my dear, believe me."

"It's hard." Eglantine paused.

"I know, I know. But you know, dear, you must think about the good times you had with your parents, the happy times."

"Like when Da would tell us the stories of the order of

the guardian owls of Ga'Hoole before we went to sleep. 'Knights' he called them."

"Yes, dear, I listened to his stories, too. He had a lovely sonorous voice, especially for a Barn Owl."

"But Mrs. P., Da thought that the stories were just legends. He didn't know they were true and that now Soren and I are here and someday we, too, shall be Guardians of Ga'Hoole. If Mum and Da only knew." Eglantine sighed deeply.

"But I think they do, dear. That's just the point. Why else would their scrooms have tried to warn Soren? They might have had unfinished business, but they knew that you and Soren and Twilight and Digger and Gylfie could finish the business, for you are almost Guardians of Ga'Hoole, are you not?"

"Well, they are. But not me — yet."

"Oh, yet!" Mrs. Plithiver swung her head as if to wipe away the word. "In your gizzard, I know you feel it. And that you are."

"Really, Mrs. Plithiver?"

"Really, Eglantine."

Eglantine returned to the hollow feeling much better. Indeed, she was almost excited about their adventure.

CHAPTER SEVEN
The Harvest Festival

At the Great Ga'Hoole Tree, there were four seasons, beginning in winter with the time of the white rain, then spring, which was known as the time of the silver rain, followed in the summer by the golden rain, and finally the autumn, which was known as the season of the copper rose. The seasons were thus called because of the vines of milkberries that cascaded from every branch of the great tree. The delicious berries of the vines made up a major part of the owls' nonmeat diet. From the ripened berries they brewed their tea, and made stews and cakes, loaves of fragrant bread, and soup. The dried berries were used for highly nutritious snacks, and as a source of instant energy as well as flavoring for other dishes.

Right now, at the time of the copper rose, was when the berries were the ripest and the plumpest for picking. During this time, the owls forsook their usual schedule and even shortened their daytime sleep so they could harvest the strands. The Ga'Hoolology ryb, a Burrowing Owl known as Dewlap, supervised the harvest. For the past week, they had all been on shifts under her command, cutting lengths of the berry vines just the right way.

"Remember, young'uns," Dewlap trilled as they flew with the strands of vines in their beaks. "No cutting below the third nodule. We must leave something so the vine shall sprout again come the time of the silver rain."

Soren and his friend Primrose, a Pygmy Owl, who had been rescued the night that Soren had arrived at the Great Ga'Hoole Tree, were flying together with a vine between them.

"She is such a bore," sighed Primrose. "Aren't you thankful that none of us got the Ga'Hoolology chaw?"

"Yes, just going to Dewlap's classes is bad enough. I was really worried that Eglantine might get the chaw."

"Never!" Primrose said. "She's perfect for search-and-rescue with her fine hearing skills. She's a natural for the chaw, I would say."

Soren, of course, could not help but wonder about their own mission to the border between Silverveil and The Barrens, which, if all went according to plan, would begin tonight just after the last of the vines had been cut.

Just then a cheer began to rise, and with the first strains of the harp, a song rang out. It was a solemn song, the "Harvest Hymn," led by Madame Plonk and Dewlap.

Dearest tree we give our thanks
for your blessings through the years.
Vines heavy with sweet berries
nourish us and quench our fears.

And in times of summer droughts,
searing heat or winters cold,
from your bounty freely given
we grow strong and we grow bold.

Let us always tend with care
your bark, your roots, your vines so fair —

And then, suddenly, a raucous song blasted out, led by Bubo.

Drink, drink to old Ga'Hoole —
boola boola boola boole!
Come along, mates, and give a tipple —
how that wine makes gizzards ripple!

Just as the song swelled with Bubo's voice leading, Otulissa swept up beside Soren and Primrose. "I can't believe Madame Plonk. She's sashaying about with a rose in her beak and wiggling her tail feathers in a most unseemly fashion. And Dewlap had hardly finished with the hymn before that coarse old owl began his vulgar song. Simply appalling."

Soren thought if he heard Otulissa say the word "appalling" one more time he might crack her on the head. Then that Spotted Owl would really see spots. But he didn't. Instead, he just turned to her and blinked. "Give it a blow, Otulissa. It's a festival for Glaux's sake. We can't be singing hymns the whole time."

"I agree," said Primrose. "Who wants a festival to be all serious? I'm hoping to pick up a few wet-poop jokes."

"Why, I never!" Otulissa said, genuinely shocked. "You know, Primrose, that wet-poop jokes are strictly forbidden at mealtimes."

"But they say all the grown-ups get very tipsy and start making them themselves."

"Well, I'm sure Strix Struma won't." Strix Struma, an elderly Spotted Owl who taught navigation, was one of the most esteemed owls of the tree. She was elegant. She was fierce. And she was revered, especially by Otulissa, who absolutely worshiped the old Spotted Owl. It was difficult, in fact, thinking of Strix Struma doing anything the least bit vulgar. The young Spotted Owl flew off in a huff toward the entrance of the Great Hollow.

As they passed through, two owls helped to part the

moss curtains as they had on the night when Soren, Gylfie, Twilight, and Digger had first arrived nearly a year before. Now, however, the Great Hollow was festooned with strands of milkberry vines that seemed almost to glow in the reflected light of hundreds of candles. The festivities had already begun and owls were swooping in flight to the music of the harp. The great grass harp stood on a balcony and was played by the nest-maid snakes who belonged to the harp guild. Their pink forms glistened as they wove themselves through the strings of the harp. Soren scanned the strings for Mrs. P., who was a sliptween. Only the most talented of the snakes were sliptweens, for they were required to jump octaves. Mrs. P. usually hung around G-flat. Ah, he spotted her!

Just then, Otulissa swept by wing to wing with Strix Struma doing a kind of stately waltz that owls called the Glaucana. Then Bubo lurched by in a jig with Madame Plonk herself. They were butting flight feathers and laughing uproariously.

"Already had a tipple, I would say." Gylfie slid into flight next to Soren. Soren was dying to say, *Yes, and we better not.* For tonight was the night that they would steal away to find the rogue smith, but not until everyone else was in their cups. Their Ga'Hoole nuts cups contained the milkberry wine or even the more strongly brewed berry mead.

Soren could not really say this in front of Primrose for she had not been included in this adventure. And he must be careful around Martin and Ruby as well. They had decided that it should only be their original band and Eglantine who went on this mission to Silverveil. But, in truth, Soren was having serious doubts about Eglantine.

The plan for getting away was fairly simple. At a certain point well into the evening, the dancing would move outside among the branches. It would be easier to slip away then. They planned to go, if possible, one by one and meet at the cliffs on the far side of the island. Owls very seldom went to that side of the island, for it lengthened any journey across the Sea of Hoolemere. But the wind this evening was light and favorable so it might not lengthen their crossing by too much.

The evening, however, seemed to drag on and on. Owls were getting tipsy, but would the dancing ever spill over to the outside? Otulissa had come up and insisted on a dance with Soren. He didn't even like to dance. He felt awkward and stupid. It wasn't like flying at all, even though it was done in the air. Now Otulissa had taken it on herself to instruct him in this silly dance called the Glauc-glauc.

"Look, Soren, it's not that hard. It's one two, glauc-glauc-glauc. Then backward one two, glauc-glauc-glauc." Otulissa was batting her eyes and shaking her tail feathers.

Great Glaux, was she flirting with him? Suddenly, he had an idea. If she was flirting with him he might as well use it to his advantage.

"You know, Otulissa, I think I could do this better if we were outside."

"Oh, that's an idea!"

Now, hopefully others would follow.

Twilight was doing the Glauc-glauc with another Great Gray, and Soren caught his eye. Twilight, always a quick study, steered his partner outside, following Soren.

Others began to fly out of the Great Hollow and weave their way through the branches in the Glauc-glauc dance. Now Eglantine was coming with another Spotted Owl. *Perfect!* Soren thought. He knew that Otulissa had a crush on the particular Spotted Owl whom Eglantine now had as her dance partner. He came from a lineage as ancient and distinguished as Otulissa's own. Soren managed to glauc-glauc-glauc across the air and through some branches to where the Spotted Owl and Eglantine were dancing.

"May I cut in and have a dance with my own sister?"

When Otulissa saw with whom she was about to be partnered, she nearly swooned midair.

Soren danced Eglantine off toward Gylfie and Digger, who were dancing with each other. Digger had a lot of smooth moves for being such a great walker, as all Bur-

rowing Owls were. He combined these with flight maneuvers in a unique way.

"Watch this, Soren. I do the Glauc-glauc with a four-
four beat. It's incredible. It's like the Glauc-glauc squared.
Ready, Gylf?"

"Ready, Diggy!" *Diggy!* This was too much. Had they all
been drinking?

"Listen!" Soren said sharply. "I think it'll be time to go
soon. Everyone's pretty much in their cups from the look
of it."

"I'll say," said Twilight, flying up to them without his
partner. "Madame Plonk has passed out."

"Passed out!" The others gasped.

"Oh, I've got to see this," said Gylfie. Before Soren
could stop her the others had followed.

Sure enough, just inside the Great Hollow in a niche
in one of the galleries there was a huge pile of white feathers. Octavia, who served as nest-maid to both Madame
Plonk and Ezylryb, was slithering along the gallery toward
her, muttering about how Madame couldn't hold her
berry wine, and it was always this way. But just at that moment, there came a roar from outside and then, "Aaah!"

"The comet!" someone cried. And its red light seemed
to flare for a brief moment and spill into the hollow, cast-
ing a fiery glow over everything. Madame Plonk's feathers

shimmered red and just in that same instant, Octavia, who had been nursing Madame Plonk, swung her head toward Soren. The old blind snake seemed to look right through him.

Does she know? Does she know what we are planning and that this might be connected with Ezylryb? A shiver ran through Soren.

"All right, it's time," he whispered to the others. "I'll leave first, then Eglantine, then Gylfie, next Digger, and last Twilight. See you at the cliffs!"

With that, Soren swept from the Great Hollow, but the entire time until the moss curtains parted, he felt the eyeless gaze of Octavia boring into him. Outside, the night seemed tinged with red. The moon, still newing, was just a sliver slipping over the horizon. In the light of the comet it looked like a battle claw dipped in blood.

CHAPTER EIGHT

Into a Night Stained Red

W here's Eglantine?" Soren said in a taut voice. "She was supposed to leave right after me." All the other owls had arrived at the cliff except Eglantine. "Do you think she got frightened?" Soren asked.

"Maybe she got caught," Gylfie offered.

"Oh, Glaux — I hope not." Soren sighed. He wondered how long they should wait.

"I hear something!" Digger said suddenly.

Owls were unusually silent fliers, all owls, that is, except for certain ones like Pygmy and Elf Owls who did not have the soft fringes called plummels at the leading edges of their flight feathers. The wing beats that Digger heard were the unmistakable sound of Primrose. Soren knew it in an instant, for he had flown behind her many a time in navigation class. What in the name of Glaux was Primrose doing here?

Eglantine, along with Primrose, slid onto the cliff and

perched beside Soren. "I know what you're going to say, Soren," she blurted out breathlessly.

But he said it anyway. "Primrose, what are you doing here?"

The Pygmy Owl shyly looked down at her talons. "I wanted to come, Soren. You helped me when I came to the great tree. You stayed with me all that first night, the night I lost my parents, my hollow, my tree, and the eggs." Primrose's parents had gone off to help out in some borderland skirmishes. They thought that she and the eggs would be safe, but a forest fire had broken out in their absence. Primrose had been rescued by owls from Ga'Hoole. But she had never seen her parents again. The truth, however, was that Primrose was from Silverveil, and Soren sensed that she wanted to go back to see if perhaps she could find her parents. This could be a distraction from their mission.

"Primrose." Soren fixed the little owl in the shine of his dark eyes.

"I know what you're going to say, Soren."

Everyone seemed to know what he was going to say, Soren thought, so why did he bother even saying it?

"I am not going to look for my parents. They are dead. I know it."

"How do you know it?" Gylfie asked.

"Do you remember the night after Trader Mags came

last summer?" Soren would never forget that night, for it was the first night that Eglantine had really been back to her old self after being rescued. It had been a beautiful summer night and then, as if in celebration of his sister's return, the sky had blossomed with colors — colors like he had never seen before. It was the night of the Aurora Glaucora, and all of the owls had flown in and out of the colors that throbbed and billowed in the sky.

"Of course, I remember that night." It was a night to remember for several reasons, one of the least happy was because on that night it had been confirmed that Ezylryb had disappeared. But in the ecstasy of the shifting colors of the sky, Soren had actually willed himself not to think about his favorite teacher.

"Well, I remember it, too, because that was the night that I saw the scrooms of my parents," Primrose said.

"What?" They all gasped.

"You saw your parents' scrooms?" Gylfie asked and there seemed to be an ache embedded deep in her voice. For although she knew that Soren had returned much saddened by his encounter with his parents' scrooms, there was something in Gylfie, just as there had been in Eglantine, that longed for one last glimpse.

"Yes," replied Primrose. "I saw them that night as we were flying through the colors of the Aurora Glaucora."

"Did they have unfinished business here on earth?" Soren asked, wondering to himself just how much unfinished scroom business they could manage on one mission.

"Not really." She paused. "Well, I suppose you could say that I was their last piece of unfinished business. They wanted me to know that during the forest fire, they knew that I had tried my best to save the eggs. They just said that there was nothing to forgive. They were proud of me. That was their unfinished business — to let me know that they were proud of me." There was a deep silence in the night as Primrose started to explain. "You see, Soren, my encounter was not at all like yours. I didn't really get to talk with my parents in that strange wordless way that you described to Eglantine."

Soren looked sharply at his sister. *Why had she gone and told Primrose all this?*

"It was much different."

"How?" Soren said, genuinely perplexed.

"You see, my parents were in glaumora."

"What?" Soren said in disbelief. "How do you know that?"

"I saw them there. They saw me. They were happy. They knew I had done my best for the eggs that never hatched. They weren't angry. They knew that I was in a good place. A place they had never quite believed in, but they now know is real. And I suddenly became so happy. It was like a river of happiness and peace flowing between us out there, in the Aurora Glaucora." Primrose's voice was barely a whisper now.

"A river of happiness," Soren said softly. No words about Metal Beak — no words at all, just happiness. He tried to imagine his parents and a river of happiness flowing between them and himself and Eglantine. Then he jerked himself back from such reveries. What he had to say next was going to be very difficult. He was going to have to refuse to have Primrose and Eglantine on this mission.

"Primrose, there will be a time when we will need you and Eglantine." He paused.

"What?" Eglantine was stunned. "You're not taking me? You promised," she whined.

"Eglantine, you are not ready. You proved this tonight by blabbing to Primrose." He then spun his head toward Primrose. "Primrose, you are certainly ready but it was our decision that the fewer the better on this mission. The less chance that we'll be missed if it is just us."

"I understand, Soren. Don't apologize."

"But what about me?" Eglantine whined again. "I'm your sister."

"Yes, and someday you will be stronger, stronger in wing and stronger in gizzard. And we shall need you, and you shall be included."

Eglantine's wings drooped by her side. Her black eyes seemed to swim with the reflected light of stars.

"We must prepare to go now," Soren said.

"Good luck," Primrose said in a full strong voice. "Be careful."

"Yes, be careful, Soren," Eglantine said softly.

"Eglantine, don't be mad. A promise is a promise. When you're ready we'll both know it."

"I could never be mad at you, Soren. Never."

"I know," he replied softly.

Soren now looked to the south. The wake of the comet was still visible. But it made for a strange light in the sky, a light that could be deceiving. He would have Twilight, whose vision for marginal conditions like these was renowned, fly in the point position. "Ready for takeoff! Twilight, fly point, Gylfie, port side. I'll fly starboard, Digger, fly tail."

They lifted off into the strangely colored night. Why was the night stained red? When he had first seen the comet a few weeks before, it had appeared red because it was dawn and the sun was just rising, but now it was night and there was no rising sun. It gave Soren the shivers to think about it and the more he did, the more the sky looked not simply rusty, but like blood. And there was another curious phenomenon. The wind was a light head wind and should have slowed them down. But, indeed, it was the reverse. It seemed as if the comet had cleared a path, created a vacuum through which they passed easily. It was as if they were being pulled instead. He was supposed to be the leader of this band. But where was he leading them, and what were they being pulled toward? Suddenly, the night seemed ominous to Soren. He felt something cold and quivering deep in his gizzard.

CHAPTER NINE

The Rogue Smith of Silverveil

Dawn was breaking. They had been flying over Silver-veil for what seemed like hours, scouring the landscape below for any sign of smoke. It was the smoke that had led them to the cave of the dying Barred Owl so many months before.

"Do you think we'll ever find him?" Soren called across from his starboard position.

"Her," Gylfie said. "It's a *her*."

"Oh, sorry, I just can't get used to a female as a black-smith."

"Well, get used to it," Gylfie said somewhat testily.

"Rotate positions," Soren called out. "Let's look for a rest spot. Crows will be up soon. We don't want a mobbing." Soren, Gylfie, Twilight, and Digger had been mobbed once before on their way to the Great Ga'Hoole Tree. It was not an experience they wished to repeat. Digger had been seriously injured. Owls flying in the daytime are not safe, except perhaps over water. Crows have a system for alerting other crows to the owls' presence and can come upon them in a swarm, often pecking out their eyes, stabbing them from beneath, and making their wings collapse. In the night, it is quite the reverse. Then it is the owls who can mob the crows. Just as Soren was about to take over the point position, Twilight spotted a big fir tree below, perfect for fetching up for a day's sleep.

"Fir tree below!"

Soren's gizzard gave a small twitch. It was a fir tree just like the one in which he and Eglantine had been hatched and had spent a brief childhood with their parents. There were countless little ceremonies, rites of passage, that marked the development of a young owl. And because of his snatching and whatever it was that had happened to Eglantine when she had fallen from the nest or perhaps been pushed by Kludd, the two young owls had missed many of these. Whenever Soren mentioned this in front of the others, they all seemed quite sympathetic, except for Twilight. Twilight had been orphaned at such a young age that he had no nest memories and prided himself on having actually skipped such folderol ceremonies, as he referred to them. Not the most modest of owls, he bragged about having learned it all on his own in what he called the Orphan School of Tough Learning, which, frankly, became quite a bore to the others.

The fragrance of the fir needles filled Soren with a great sense of longing. He yearned for his parents, not the scrooms, but his real, live parents.

Soren could not let himself give in to these feelings. "Before we take a snooze, we have to plan." Action, Soren always felt, was the best remedy for sad feelings. "I've been thinking that when we met the Barred Owl, he was not just on a border, he was really on a point where the corners of four borders touched, those of Kuneer, Ambala, The Beaks, and Tyto."

"A convergence point," Gylfie offered.

"Yes, I think we should look for such a point of convergence. Gylfie, you're the navigator. You've studied the map. Which way should we head?"

"Well, for a convergence we need to head toward the point where Silverveil, the Shadow Forest, and The Barrens meet," Gylfie said. "Tonight, when the constellation of the Great Glaux rises, we have to fly two degrees off its westerly wing, just between that and the claw of the Little Raccoon."

"All right, everyone get a good rest. We'll leave at First Black," Soren said.

Three hours after First Black they had still seen nothing. They had been in the region of the convergence for two hours. Soren told himself he could not get discouraged. He was the leader of this band. If the owls sensed he was discouraged, then their spirits, too, would begin to fall. They could not fail. Too much was at stake.

Digger flew up to Soren. "Permission for low-level surveillance, Soren."

"What for?"

"Tracking, Soren. I'm used to low-level flight for finding downed owls and anything else on the ground. Look at me. We blend in with everything, desert sand and fallen leaves in autumn. And I can fly slow, really slow, noisy but slow. And," he paused, "I can walk!"

"All right, but I expect you back within the quarter hour."

"Yes, Captain."

Captain! He wanted to cry out, *Don't call me Captain. Only Ezylryb can be called Captain.*

Soren watched as Digger went into a plunging dive.

As he neared the ground, Digger began a slow survey, first for any sign of caves, or scattered coals that might indicate the presence of a rogue smith. When he found no caves, he wondered if a blacksmith would ever build a fire in a clearing. Possibly. Then, of course, there was the fact that this blacksmith was a Snowy Owl. Pure white. She should certainly show up on a night like this. With the moon far from full and still just newing, the night was very black. Perfect for seeing white.

The quarter of an hour was running out. Digger became more determined than ever, more intense in his search. Scanning by rotating his head as he had been taught to do in tracking, he dodged bushes, tree trunks, rocks, and other ground obstacles just in the nick of time. He sensed them almost before he got to them. But he hadn't sensed the large black mound ahead. Neither rock nor shrub nor trunk, the mound suddenly sprung to life.

"Watch where you're going, idiot!"

Digger's gizzard froze.

"Racdrops!" Another scream from the mound. Digger felt something soft and then there was a small blizzard of sooty particles. He tumbled head over talons and this smothering cloud seemed to follow him. They were rolling down a small incline.

"Glaux almighty! You splat-brained idiot!" A scathing rant rang out. Digger had never heard such a stream of swears. The vilest curses scalded the night air and rained down on his ears. Bubo was no match. "Great stinkin' Glaux, I might have known — a Burrowing Owl with most likely a small burrow where your brain should be. What happened? Did it fall out?"

"I beg your racdrop pardon! You wretched piece of wet poop." Digger drew himself up to his full height. He surprised himself with his own swearing.

"Wet poop! I'll splat you."

This isn't working, Digger suddenly thought. He could not stand here trading insults with this sooty black thing. "Truce," he said. The creature stopped and stood still. "Who are you? What are you?" Digger asked.

"A bird, you darned fool."

"A bird?"

"An owl. A Snowy at that."

"Snowy!" Digger gasped and nearly laughed out loud. "You are the blackest Snowy I have ever seen."

"What did you expect? I'm a blacksmith, idiot!"

It was music to Digger's ears. "A blacksmith," he said, his voice drenched in awe and relief. "The rogue smith of Silverveil?" Digger asked softly.

"What business is that of yours? You want battle claws? I rarely make them for Burrowing Owls. They're lousy fliers. It's a waste."

Digger swallowed his anger at this insult. "No, no, Bubo told us about you."

"Bubo!" the owl suddenly exploded. "You're from Ga'Hoole? Bubo sent you here?"

"Not exactly,"

"What does that mean?" The Snowy narrowed her eyes until they were two yellow slits.

"Uh . . . I better go get my friends," Digger stammered and quickly took off.

CHAPTER TEN
The Story of the Rogue Smith

Soren blinked as he and the three other owls lighted down. Digger had not been kidding when he had said that this was the blackest Snowy he had ever seen.

"So what brings you here, young'uns? I take it that you're not here on a sanctioned visit."

Gylfie was the only one who knew what the word "sanctioned" meant. So she answered, "No, this is not an official visit. As a matter of fact —"

The black Snowy finished her thought. "Sneaked away, didya? A little escapade, I imagine? Dreams of glory? Huh?"

Soren fluffed up his feathers in a bristle of annoyance. "It is not an escapade. It is a mission, and we do not dream of glory. We hope for peace, for we have been warned."

"Warned of what?" the smith said with a slight note of disdain.

This owl frinks me off! Soren took a deep breath. "Metal Beak."

A tremor went through the black Snowy and little puffs of coal dust sifted down from her feathers. "What'-cha doin' messin' with that creep for? He ain't around these parts. And I'll have you know, I don't sell to him. Not on your life. Not on my life. Course that's a risk in itself, not selling to him."

"What do you know about him?" Gylfie asked.

"Very little. I steer clear of him and his gang. And I advise you to as well."

"Gang?" Soren said.

"Yeah, gang. Don't know how many."

"Is he part of St. Aggie's?" Gylfie asked.

"You only wish," the black Snowy said. And with these words, Soren, Twilight, Gylfie, and Digger froze in terror. For, in fact, these were the very same words spoken by the dying Barred Owl, his last words when Gylfie had asked him if it was St. Aggie's that had mortally wounded him. For these four owls to imagine anything worse than St. Aggie's was terrifying. Now, however, it seemed that the "you only wish" could be tied to Metal Beak. And there was not just one of them but possibly many.

"Did you know about the murder of the Barred Owl of The Beaks?" Twilight asked.

"I heard a thing or two about it. I don't go poking into things that ain't my business. Not my way." Soren remembered what Bubo had said about rogue smiths never attaching themselves to any kingdom.

"Where's your forge?" Gylfie asked looking around.

"Not here."

This is one tough owl, thought Soren. *Almost like she's not used to talking.* But then Digger had said she could swear like nobody's business. Used words that he had never even heard Bubo use. That was something — an owl who could out-curse Bubo. Although the owl hadn't said that much, there was something oddly familiar in her tone. Soren couldn't place it, however.

"Well, may I be so bold as to ask where your forge is?" Gylfie persisted. *Good for you, Gylf.* This was one of the advantages of being small, Soren thought. No one ever expected you to be bold or aggressive.

"Yonder!" The smith turned her head and indicated somewhere behind her shoulder.

"Might we see it?" Gylfie took a tiny step forward. The black Snowy towered over her, looked down and blinked.

"Why?"

"Because we're interested. We've never seen a rogue smith's forge before."

The Snowy paused as if to consider if this was an adequate reason. "It ain't fancy like Bubo's."

"That doesn't matter," Twilight said. "Do we look

fancy?" Twilight puffed himself up. The inverted curves of white feathers that swept from his brow framed his eyes and beak and made his fierce glare even fiercer. He looked anything but fancy.

The black Snowy turned to Gylfie. "You're small to be out here with this bunch of hooligans."

"We're not hooligans, ma'am," Gylfie replied.

"Why'd you call me that?" The smith glared at Gylfie but the Elf Owl stood her ground firmly and met the blazing yellow gaze.

Uh-oh, thought Soren. *This bird does not like being called ma'am.* Soren remembered what Bubo had said about the rogue smiths being loners. How had Bubo put it? *They likes living wild.* Being called ma'am — or sir, for that matter, if it were a male — would prick their gizzards.

"We aren't hooligans. We are a band. Soren here is like a brother to me. We escaped from St. Aggie's together. Shortly after we escaped, we met up with Twilight and Digger. Soon we shall have our Guardian ceremony and become true Guardians of Ga'Hoole." Gylfie turned and swept her wing toward the three other owls who seemed almost spellbound by her words. "And I called you 'ma'am' because underneath all that coal dust, I know there is a beautiful Snowy. As beautiful as the most beautiful Snowy of the great tree, Madame Plonk."

At that, the smith seemed to choke and then tears began to leak from her eyes. *That's it!* That's who the smith reminded Soren of. The tone of her voice, it was the same melodic sound, the same *pling* that he heard in Madame Plonk's voice each night when she sang the "Night Is Done" song.

"How did you guess I was Brunwella's sister?"

"You mean Madame Plonk? Is that her name?" Soren asked.

"Yes. Come, follow me to the forge, young'uns. I'll tell you the story. I have some fresh voles. Mind you, I don't roast them here like you do in the Great Tree."

"Don't worry," Soren said. "I fly weather and colliering with Ezylryb — or did — and we always have to take our meat raw."

"Oh, yes. I heard about Ezylryb. No sign of him yet?"

"No," said Soren sadly as they flew the short distance to the forge.

"Dear old fellow. We go back, way back."

Soren wondered what the Snowy meant by that? Well, perhaps they would soon find out.

"What is this?" Digger asked as the band lighted down in the stone ruins. There were two-and-a-half walls of ancient stone that had been neatly stacked upon one another. Old vines crawled over them and in the center was the pit where the smith had her fire. On one of the walls, a new set of battle claws and a helm hung. Soren could see that the work was very fine, every bit as good as Bubo's.

"It used to be a walled garden. At least, that's what I think. Maybe part of a castle."

"The Others?" Soren asked.

"Oh, you know about the Others do you?" the smith asked.

"Just a little, from the books in the library when I was reading about castles and churches and barns. Being a Barn Owl, it interested me. I just know that they were creatures from long, long ago, and they weren't owls or birds or like any other animals we've ever seen."

"That they warn't. Did you know that not only did they not have wings or feathers, but that they had two long sticks for legs that were just for walking."

"That's all?" Digger said. This, of course, interested him, being a Burrowing Owl who walked as well as he flew. But he certainly preferred having the option to do either one. "How did they get along?"

"Not that well, apparently. They're gone now. In addition to no feathers, they didn't have fur."

"Well, no wonder they didn't last," Twilight snorted.

"Rocks, they had rocks," the Snowy said.

"Rocks? What can you do with a rock?" Twilight muttered.

"Plenty," the Snowy replied. "They built with them — castles, walled gardens."

"Why would anyone want to wall in a garden?" Digger asked, thinking of the lovely gardens that were planted around the Great Ga'Hoole Tree that seemed to meet up in a seamless way with the ferns and wildflowers of the forest.

"Don't ask me," the Snowy said.

The Snowy had begun to lay out some freshly killed voles and a couple of ground squirrels.

She chuckled to herself as if she had discovered something terribly amusing and a light drift of coal dust sprinkled down on her face.

"So it's hard for you all to believe that I am the famous Madame Plonk's sister, eh?"

"To put it mildly," Gylfie replied.

"She's a good soul but she's very different from me. We were born, my sister and I, deep in the Northern Kingdoms, far beyond the Ice Narrows, on the eastern coast of the Everwinter Sea. Some say that is where Snowy Owls originated. But there were others up there. Your teacher Ezylryb came from an island near where I was born. And he's a Screech Owl. Anyhow, there was always a lot of fighting up in those parts. Warring clans. The fiercest warriors came out of the region of the Everwinter Sea. My father and my mother being two of them. But despite their war-like ways, my parents were artists, and for generations the line of Plonk singers were renowned. For thousands of years in every community, in every kingdom, there has been a Plonk singer. But the singer for the Great Ga'Hoole Tree is an inherited position and it is given to only one Snowy in each generation — the one considered the finest. Well, that was my sister, Brunwella. I could have lived with that, but what I couldn't live with was my stepmother.

"After my mum was killed in the Battle of the Ice Talons — the last battle in the War of the Ice Claws — my da found a new mate, a horrible old Snowy. She treated me like seagull splat. And, of course, fussed over my sister because my sister was going to be the singer for the great tree. I had to leave. Even Brunwella saw that it was impossible for me to continue in the hollow. My father, however, was besotted with this female. She could do no wrong. I wasn't sure where to go. For some reason, I felt it was important for me not only to get as far away as possible from my family but to take up a whole new line of work. My voice wasn't bad. But not nearly as good as that of most Plonks which, of course, meant it was a lot better than anyone else's. But I wanted no part of it. And I wasn't as lovely-looking as my sister. I was given to gray scale, which made for unsightly splotches where the feathers fell off. As a matter of fact, my stepmother used to call me 'Splotch.'"

"How mean!" Gylfie said. "What is your real name?"

Will she say what it is? Soren thought. He looked at her closely.

"My true name?"

"Yes," Gylfie said in a barely audible voice. It was as if she sensed she had ventured into forbidden territory.

"That is for me to know, and only me."

But what about your sister? Soren thought. *Doesn't she know your true name? And what is the difference between a true name and a real name? Is there a difference?*

"So, as I was saying, I was looking for something new and different. I really wanted to separate myself from the Plonks. My sister had been good to me, but my father seemed not to care. I really had no one else to turn to. So I just left. I flew about in the Northern Kingdoms for a year or more, and then I came upon Octavia. You know Octavia, don't you?"

"Of course," they all cried.

"She's Ezylryb's and your sister's nest-maid snake," said Soren.

"Oh, she's working for my sister now, is she? Well, she's a good old soul. I, of course, met her before she was blind."

The owls all gasped in disbelief.

"You mean," said Gylfie, "she wasn't born blind?"

"I had heard a rumor that she had not been born blind, but I really didn't believe it. I thought all nest-maid snakes were born blind," Soren said.

"They are — except for Octavia. Haven't you noticed that she's not rosy-scaled like the others?"

Soren had noticed and wondered about Octavia's pale greenish-blue scales.

"But that's a whole other story. It was Octavia who told me about a rogue smith on the island of Dark Fowl, a desolate place that is lashed constantly by ice storms and gales, rocky, not a tree, not a blade of grass. But this smith was supposed to be one of the most superb blacksmiths on earth. So I went there. I wanted to learn how to make battle claws. I wanted to avenge my mother's death. I had a dream of making battle claws that would slice to shreds the clan that had killed my mum. I had the fire in my gizzard as they say. Smithing came naturally to me, more natural than singing, I'll tell you." She sighed and seemed to reflect happily for a moment. "And I did kill my stepmum with some magnificent claws I made."

"You killed your stepmother?" Twilight had swollen up

with excitement. Never having even known his own parents he had no romantic notions in general about them, and an evil stepmother set his gizzard to boiling. Then the Great Gray looked down at his talons in what Soren thought was a pathetic display of shyness — for shy was the last thing that Twilight was. "I don't want you to think I'm a violent sort of bird."

"Ha!" the other three owls laughed.

"Well, I'm not!" Twilight said stubbornly and blinked at his mates.

However, any one of them could see the Great Gray could hardly contain himself.

"But how'd you do it? Quick slice to the gullet? How? Talon to talon? Stab with the beak to the nether down?"

"I don't care about how," Soren interrupted. "But why? I mean, I know she was bad, but that bad?"

"She betrayed my father. Turned out she was a slipgizzle for the other clan. Had planned to marry him from the start — as soon as they got rid of Mum."

"How did you learn this?" Digger asked.

"I had my ways. Working for a master rogue smith you find out a lot of things. All sorts come to you by the by."

Digger looked at the coal-dusted Snowy carefully. "Did Octavia have something do with this? Or maybe —" But the blacksmith cut him off.

Cut Digger off too quickly, Soren observed. Then the rogue smith of Silverveil seemed to clam up. Oh, she was very hospitable, giving them the best parts of the voles and making sure that they had comfortable perches for the day.

Soren did have one more question for her but something kept him from asking it. He wondered, however, if the rogue smith of Silverveil thought that Metal Beak was in any way connected with Ezylryb's disappearance. Soren wrestled with his question all through their daytime sleep and finally, just before First Black when he noticed that the Snowy was stirring, he decided he just had to ask.

He flew down to where the blacksmith was taking some coals from a niche in the wall to build up her forging fire.

"I knew you'd come and ask," the Snowy Owl said. Soren blinked. "You want to know if Metal Beak had something to do with Ezylryb."

"Yes. How did you know?"

"Never mind that," she snapped. "The fact is I'm not sure, but Ezylryb, well, how to explain? Ezylryb has a past. He is a legend. He does have enemies."

"Enemies?" This was unbelievable to Soren. Ezylryb never went into battle. This was a well-known fact at the great tree. He might be gruff, but he was the most nonviolent owl imaginable. How could such an owl have enemies? He didn't even own battle claws. In fact, he once said he despised them. Thought the owl kingdoms were becoming much too dependent on them. "Give them books, give them tasty milkberry tarts, teach them to cook, teach them the ways of Ga'Hoole," he had said to the owl parliament, "and every cantankerous owl will be on our side." *Ezylryb violent! It's absurd.*

"One last question," Soren said.

"Yes?"

"Why do they call that owl Metal Beak?"

"He got half his face torn off in a battle. A rogue smith had to make him a mask and a new beak."

Soren felt as if he might be sick.

CHAPTER ELEVEN
Flint Mops

I t's the part about Octavia not being born blind that absolutely blows my gizzard," Gylfie was saying.

"It's the enemies thing for me," Digger said. "It's unbelievable that the rogue smith told Soren that Ezylryb has enemies, and that's why Metal Beak might be connected to his disappearance."

"I know," Soren said, "that's what gets me, too."

They had returned to the great tree. No one seemed to have missed them and now, in their hollow, Gylfie, Twilight, Soren, and Digger were reviewing and telling Eglantine all they had learned from the rogue smith of Silverveil. They really weren't sure if they had learned that much. They were, in truth, still quite mystified. Were they any closer to Metal Beak? Was there any chance of them actually being able to do something about the scrooms' warning?

"Tell me about the rogue smith's forge again?" This was about the fourth time Eglantine had asked. For some reason, she was fascinated by their description of this place. So Soren began once more to describe how the stones were stacked in walls, walls that the Snowy thought might have enclosed a garden.

"Did she say anything else?"

Twilight sighed as if he was extremely bored with this conversation, but Soren felt that answering Eglantine's interminable questions was the least he could do for his little sister after making her stay back at the tree.

"What do you mean by anything else?"

"Did she say what it might have been other than a garden?"

"Well, now that I remember she actually did say that it could have been a walled garden that was part of a castle."

"A castle!" Eglantine's eyes blinked.

"You know, one of those things that the Others built."

"Yes, I know. . . ." Eglantine responded in a tremulous voice.

She suddenly seemed very agitated. "What's wrong, Eglantine?" Soren asked.

"I'm not sure. It's just that the way you described those stones, those walls remind me of something."

Soren suddenly remembered that when Eglantine was still in her state of shock after her rescue and could not even recognize him, her own brother, that it was a colorful piece of isinglass, or mica, as it was also called, that had jolted Eglantine out of her numbed state. Mags, the magpie trader who sometimes came to the tree with her odd bits scavenged from various journeys, had brought the fragment. When someone had held the isinglass up to the moon, the thin, nearly translucent piece of stone had shimmered and, suddenly, Eglantine had started shaking and screaming, "The Place! The Place!" But no one could ever figure out quite what place she was talking about, and until now Soren hadn't really thought about it that much. At the time, he hadn't thought it really mattered. After all, his sister had recognized him and had quickly come around to her old self. But now, Soren wondered why his description of these walls reminded her of something. He hadn't the slightest idea. He sent Gylfie down for some milkberry tea, thinking that it might calm Eglantine enough for her to get to sleep. He hated to see his sister so distraught.

But it was Gylfie, returning with a small flask of milkberry tea in her talons, who was truly distraught.

"We've been discovered!"

"What?" Soren almost shrieked. "What are you talking about?"

"I didn't tell, I swear!" Eglantine spoke in a desperate whisper.

"Of course you didn't. I trust you, Eglantine. I know you'd never tell." Eglantine seemed to almost melt, not just in relief but with the simple knowledge of her brother's trust in her. She had felt she was just about useless, good for nothing of importance. But that Soren trusted her meant everything.

At that very moment, Primrose flew into their hollow. "It wasn't Eglantine, and it wasn't me."

"Otulissa!" Twilight hissed.

"No, not Otulissa. Dewlap."

"Dewlap!" They all gasped. Dewlap was the Burrowing Owl who was head of the Ga'Hoolology chaw, generally thought to be the most boring chaw in the entire tree. It was devoted to understanding the physiology and natural processes of the great tree where they lived, which sustained their lives. And even if you were not in a particular chaw, you were still required to take classes in that subject.

"Oh, racdrops!" Twilight slapped the air with his feathers, causing a hearty gust to sweep through the hollow. "Dewlap gave me a flint mop for acting up in class the other day. I completely forgot." Twilight was always getting into trouble in Ga'Hoolology. It was easy as it was so boring. In fact, the other owls lived for Twilight's antics during that class. He was the only source of relief from boredom. "I was supposed to go help her bury pellets at tween time."

Tween time was the time between the last drop of sun and the first shadows of the evening.

"Well, she started snooping around and found all of you gone," Primrose said.

"Do they know where we were?" Soren asked.

Gylfie shrugged. "I don't know. But the four of us are to report immediately to Boron and Barran." Gylfie paused. "In the parliament."

"Oh, Glaux! In front of everyone?" Digger said. There were in all eleven owls who made up the governing body of the Great Ga'Hoole Tree known as the parliament. They decided to which chaws the new owls, after a period of general training and education, would be assigned. They planned the precise dates on which the milkberries would be harvested. They were in charge of all missions of diplomacy, war, and, most important, support to owls or groups of owls in need. They supervised all the many ceremonies and festivals of the great tree and settled all arguments. They also decided on appropriate "flint mops," as they were called, since there was no real word for "punish" or "punishment" in the language of the owls of Ga'Hoole. Owls were never struck, hit, bitten, locked up, or given less food. They did not even believe in taking away privileges such as attending parties or festivities or banquets. What they did believe in was the flint mop. Flint stone was the most valuable tool the owls of Ga'Hoole had. It was with their flint stones that they ignited their fires. The word flint had, over the years, become a synonym for anything of great value. To say something was flinty or had flint meant it had real worth. Therefore to be a flint mopper was to be someone who scorned the value of something. And if you scorned the value of something, you were required to pay back what you had taken away. Thus, the term for the payback came to be known as a "flint mop" as well. A flint mop was as close as owls came to the word punishment. And the flint mop in Twilight's case was helping Dewlap, the Ga'Hoolology ryb, bury pellets which nourished the roots of the tree.

"So we have to go to the parliament right now?" Soren asked.

"Right now." Gylfie nodded. "And I don't think we should be late."

"Enter!" It was the loud resonant hoot of Boron through the bark doors of the parliament hollow. This hollow was one of the few that had actual doors, for the business of the parliament was often top secret. Although Twilight, Soren, Gylfie, and Digger had, in fact, discovered a place deep within the tangled roots of the tree where something strange happened to the timber of the trunk just above and the voices of the parliament owls could be heard. Sometimes the four owls listened in. Had this been found out it might be considered worse than what they had done now. Although Soren was still not sure what they had done that was so bad. Yes, they had gone away during the harvest festival — but was that really all that bad? It was bad if it had been found out where they had gone perhaps, but the only one who could really be considered a flint mopper was Twilight, who had completely forgotten to do his flint mop.

Only three owls of the parliament were perched on the white birch branch that had been bent into a half circle. There was Boron, his mate, Barran, and Dewlap. He supposed he should be relieved that there were just three and not the entire parliament. And, insofar that the only other owl present besides the monarchs was Dewlap, this might mean that indeed the worst error was Twilight's forgetting his flint mop.

"Young'uns," Barran began. "It was brought to our attention by the good ryb Dewlap that Twilight was absent from his flint-mopping tasks of burying pellets, which nourishes our great tree. Upon further investigation, it was found out that all four of you, the entire 'band' as you are known, had left the tree on the night of the festivities. So not only was Twilight unavailable for flint mopping but the rest of you could not participate in the sorting and grading of milkberries, as is customary after the harvest festivities, not to mention the award ceremonies, which follow the sorting, for those who have distinugished themselves at the harvest through their diligence."

Sorting, grading awards? Soren had never heard about all this. He stole a look at Gylfie who appeared equally bewildered.

Then Barran, as if reading their minds, continued, "Yes, young'uns, there are things you do not yet know about — practices and ceremonies that we have here at the Great Ga'Hoole Tree. For example, Soren, it was while you were gone that we had a First-Meat-on-Bones ceremony for your sister, Eglantine, and other young'uns from the Great Downing who had missed that owl stone event." An owl stone event was one that was considered of great significance in the development of a young owl. The First-Meat-on-Bones ceremony was one of the most important of all the ceremonies that marked a young owl's passage through life from hatchling to fully fledged flier to adept hunter. Boron and Barran felt that even though owls like Eglantine had long been eating Meat on Bones because they had been orphaned early on and missed this ceremony with their parents, it was still important to have these moments recognized. "Better late than never," Barran always said.

"I missed Eglantine's Meat-on-Bones!" A sob seemed to swell in Soren's gizzard. "Why . . . why . . ." he stammered.

"Why didn't she tell you about it?" Barran asked. Then she proceeded to answer her own question. "Because isn't it always a surprise when your parents come home with that first whole vole or ground squirrel and say 'Beak up! Down the gullet!'? No more of their stripping out the bones like when you were a baby. So why shouldn't it be a surprise here?"

Soren merely blinked. Tears filled his eyes, and the big old Snowy blurred like a cloud. "But she didn't even tell me about it when I got back."

"Eglantine is a sensitive young owl. I'm sure she knew that you would have felt awful for missing her First-Meat-on-Bones ceremony, and the last thing your sister would want is for you to feel bad. She loves you too much, Soren."

Soren's wings hung limply by his side. He felt positively horrible.

"Now, young'uns," Boron had begun to speak for the first time since saying enter.

Oh, Glaux. He's going to ask us where we've been, Soren thought.

"You were off looking for Ezylryb, I'd wager?" Soren nodded. "Well, that's to be expected."

Dewlap suddenly swelled up in a puff of indignation. "I beg to differ, Boron, but duty is what is expected."

"Oh, you're right. You're right, of course." But Soren sensed that Boron did not think that the boring Burrowing Owl was *exactly* right. Maybe they'd get off with just a light flint mop but, more important, maybe Boron would not ask them where they had been.

"Where have you been?" squawked Dewlap.

"It doesn't really matter where," Boron spoke now. "What matters is that in going away, the band missed the sorting and grading of the milkberries. Soren missed his sister's First-Meat-on-Bones ceremony, and Twilight missed his flint mop for you. Thus, the tree suffered as a whole."

"I would say," Dewlap's voice thundered, "it's payback time! The four of you are on pellet-burying detail for the next three days, twice a day."

As they flew back to their hollow from the parliament, Soren muttered under his breath to the others, "We can't complain. . . . We can't complain. . . . We got off light."

"Light? You call having to bury pellets a 'light' flint mop?" Twilight hissed.

"Look," Gylfie said, "it was because you forgot your

flint mop that we were discovered in the first place. So just shut your beak."

"You know," Digger was saying, "in spite of my being a Burrowing Owl and Dewlap being a Burrowing Owl, I feel I have nothing in common with that old hoot."

"How could you?" Gylfie asked. "She is so boring."

"And mean," Soren added.

The others blinked. They had never thought of Dewlap as mean, just boring. So had Soren until Dewlap had squawked, and he had seen a weird greenish glimmer in her yellow eyes that seemed to mask a stingy gizzard. Soren's mother had always told him that it was a stingy and envious gizzard that made owls mean. His mother had said that envy and stinginess were the worst faults an owl could have. Her words came back to him: *There is never any call for envy or stinginess in owls, Soren. We have the sky, we have the great forests and the trees. We are the most beautiful fliers on earth. Why would we envy any other bird or animal?*

CHAPTER TWELVE

Rusty Claws

By the time the four owls had returned to their hollow, Eglantine had fallen sound asleep. And soon the rest were also sleeping. Eglantine was twitching nervously in her sleep. She had seemed upset ever since they had told her about the walled garden of the forge.

Soren couldn't think about any of that now. There was still this dreadful unfinished business of Metal Beak and the "you only wish." A horrid image if there ever was one — a half-faceless owl flying around slaughtering creatures. Then again, there was just getting through the flint mop for Dewlap. Gylfie stirred and Soren saw that she was awake, too.

"Gylfie, why do you think Boron and Barran didn't ask us where we had been?"

"They knew that it had something to do with Ezylryb. They know how you feel about him. They didn't have to know exactly where you went."

"You know," Soren said slowly, "I have the feeling that

in some way Octavia might be important to all that stuff the rogue smith of Silverveil told us."

"How?" Gylfie asked in her usual practical way. "What's the link?"

"I feel it in my gizzard," Soren continued, thinking aloud, "that she somehow is connected to Ezylryb's past when perhaps he was a different kind of owl."

"Different?" Gylfie asked.

"Remember how the Snowy told us that she met Octavia before she was blind?" Gylfie nodded. "And it was Octavia who told her about the Dark Fowl Island where the master blacksmith nested. There's a connection there, a link with Ezylryb. Did Ezylryb know her then, too, before she was blind? And the rogue smith said they came here together years and years ago. She was blind then, but what was she really before that? What did she do for Ezylryb? How does a snake know about a forge on an island that makes battle claws?"

"What are you suggesting we do, Soren?" Gylfie asked.

He turned and looked at his best friend in all the world, the little Elf Owl with whom he had already endured so much. Could he ask her to do this? He knew it would shock her. He took a deep breath and then told her what he wanted to do. "I am suggesting that we get into Ezylryb's hollow when Octavia is not around."

Gylfie gasped so loud that she almost woke Twilight. "Soren, I can't believe it. That's trespassing, snooping, spying, and Ezylryb is your favorite teacher. It's so . . . so . . ."

"Scummy," Soren offered.

"Well, yes," Gylfie nodded. "I was going to say unethical. But yeah, 'scummy' just about sums it up. Soren, you surprise me. I mean, that's really asking for a flint mop."

"Who cares about flint mopping? This is life or death. If we can discover something that would help us find and save Ezylryb, it can't be scummy, unflecktual."

"Unflecktual!" Gylfie whispered hoarsely. "Flecks, Soren? Do you think this is connected with flecks?"

Soren blinked. He had meant to say that word Gylfie had used — unethical. But it had come out wrong. Still it was just a slip of the beak. But was it connected with the flecks in some way? There was a web being spun here. He could feel them all being reeled in, and at the center of the web sat a spider with a Metal Beak.

"I have to go," Soren said.

"I won't let you go without me," Gylfie said.

"It should only be the two of us."

"No," Digger suddenly spoke up.

"You awake?" Gylfie asked.

"I just woke up. Listen, I want to be in on this. You'll need a lookout. I'll stand guard. What are you two going to do if Octavia slithers in? I could distract her long enough for you to get out. Ezylryb does have a few sky ports in his hollow, doesn't he?" Sky ports were the openings directly to the outside of the tree from which the owls could fly from their hollows. There were smaller holes called trunk ports which the nest-maids usually came through.

"Of course," Soren replied.

So it was set. They would go the next day just after tween time and their flint mop for Dewlap, during harp practice. Octavia, as a member of the harp guild, would be attending.

"Gylfie! My dear, that hole is simply not deep enough." Dewlap came up to the Elf Owl. "Here, let me demonstrate. And don't use that excuse of being an Elf Owl and your beak being too tiny. One of my best chaw members ever was an Elf Owl. She dug exquisite holes."

"Doesn't she ever sleep?" Digger said under his breath at tween time as the four owls poked holes with their beaks in the soil to bury the pellets.

When the first chords of the harp rang out, they all breathed a sigh of relief. Their flint mop was done for now. And the investigation of Ezylryb's hollow could begin. The other owls were still sleeping, for during these first days following the harvest festival, the owls tended to rouse themselves later. Soren, Gylfie, and Digger made their way to Ezylryb's hollow. Located in one of the highest parts of the tree, the hollow was the only one facing the northwest, the direction of the cold prevailing wind that most owls did not fancy. But, of course, Ezylryb was not most owls. And perhaps he liked facing the direction of the Northern Kingdoms from which he had come.

As soon as they entered the hollow, Digger took up his lookout position at the trunk port. He tried to take in as much as he could of the old teacher's quarters, which appeared to have hundreds of books and maps, but Soren and Gylfie hurried him along to his watch post.

"Where do we begin?" Soren asked, looking at all the piles of papers, charts, maps, and infinite numbers of gizmos that Ezylryb had to help him interpret weather patterns. There was a vial of sand that he often hung outside his hollow, which registered the moisture in the air. There was another vial of quicksilver to gauge atmospheric pressure changes. There were at least twenty wind indicators. Ezylryb was always experimenting with new wind indicators that used feathers sometimes plucked from his own body, but it was usually a molted one from some very young owl who had just shed its baby down.

"It would be easier to know where to begin if we knew exactly what we were looking for," Gylfie replied, lighting down on a dangerously tilting stack of books.

Soren just sighed. There was something so sad about the hollow. In the month or so before the Great Downing, Ezylryb had taken to inviting members of the weather chaw to his hollow to share tea. The old ryb would talk about his latest weather theories or inventions for interpreting weather. But now the coals in his grate were cold. The plates of his favorite snack food, dried caterpillars, went untouched and a fine layer of dust had settled on all the books.

Soren knew that off of this main parlor of Ezylryb's hollow there was a smaller one where he slept. Gylfie had already flown into it. So Soren followed her. "Anything here?"

"Practically nothing," Gylfie replied.

In definite contrast to the parlor, the sleeping hollow was sparsely furnished to the point of austerity. There was a bed, a mixture of down with generous portions of Ga'Hoolian moss known for its fleecy quality. By the bed stood a small table with a slender volume of poems atop another large leather-bound volume. Soren peered at the book.

"What's the book?" Gylfie asked.

"Something called *Sonnets of the Northern Kingdoms,* by Lyze of Kiel."

"Whoop-de-doo," Gylfie said. "Sounds exciting, doesn't it?"

"Well, you know Ezylryb. Everyone says he is the best scholar here. He likes all this weird obscure stuff. It's not all just weather science with him."

"What's the other book?" Gylfie asked.

Soren moved the poetry volume. "I can hardly read the title, this book is so ancient." The leather had crackled into fine lines and the gold leaf in which the title had been written had nearly flaked away. But underneath was the faint impression of an outline of the embossed letters. Soren, looking hard at the letters, spoke slowly. "*Sagas of the North Kingdoms: The History of the War of the Ice Claws* by Lyze of Kiel."

"Talented fellow, I guess," Gylfie said. "I mean, sonnets and war history." Gylfie was talking as she flitted here and there in the almost bare chamber. "What's this?" she said suddenly.

"What's what?" Soren asked. "Oh, it looks like a perch. Must be for his exercises or something."

"No, I don't think so." And at the moment Gylfie lighted down on the perch, it fell from the wall. The Elf Owl tumbled through the air and landed lightly on her small talons. "Some perch! Can't even hold an Elf Owl like me."

Soren blinked in dismay. That was weird. Where the perch had been was a hole. Soren flew up to the hole and then, using fast, scooping motions of his wings and by angling his tail, he managed to tread the air in order to hover. *Glaux! I wish I were a hummingbird!* he thought. Hovering in a tight space for a bird of Soren's size was no easy matter. "Gylfie, get over here and hover. You're smaller. You can do this better than I can. Peek into that hole. I see something."

"You do?" Gylfie had flown up as Soren backed off. Now Gylfie hovered and then suddenly poked her beak in and within a fraction of a second came back with a string clutched in it. It was a long string and it was firmly attached to something in the hole.

"Pull it!" said Soren.

Gylfie gave a little tug. "I can't, you're stronger."

So Soren came up and gave a yank. There was a creak and suddenly a door, previously invisible, opened. The owls blinked at each other. There was no need to ask if they should or should not go in. Their minds were instantly made up. Soren entered first. It was dark but, of course, darkness never bothered an owl. They could actually see better in the dark. They made their way through a very narrow corridor. Flying through it was almost impossible even for an Elf Owl. Soon, however, the corridor widened and they found themselves standing in another hollow, about the same size as Ezylryb's sleeping quarters.

A secret chamber, thought Soren. Then both owls blinked in astonishment.

"Soren, do you see what I see?"

"I certainly do!"

Hanging on the wall in front of them was a pair of ancient, rusted battle claws. *Yes, a secret chamber for hiding secrets.* Soren now thought of his last conversation with the rogue smith of Silverveil. The words came back to him: *Ezylryb has a past. He is a legend. He does have enemies.*

How shocked Soren had been. How unbelievable it was to him that the most nonviolent owl on earth could ever have an enemy. Ezylryb, the owl who had the greatest contempt for battle claws!

"Well, will you look at these claws! Holy Glaux!" Gylfie had flown up close to them. "Makes my gizzard wilt to even be this close. Soren you won't believe this. These suckers are deadly. They've got jagged edges. Glaux almighty. Come up here and look at them."

"No!" Soren said. He couldn't stand the thought of his teacher — his hero — wearing those. Killing. He himself had killed before. He had helped kill the bobcat in the forest of The Beaks, and he had helped kill the top lieutenants of St. Aggie's, Jatt and Jutt, when the two Long-Eared cousins had attacked them in the Desert of Kuneer. But this was different somehow. This was like being a professional killer. Yes. What had they called those owls he had heard about — Hireclaws? They hired out to anyone to fight and kill. That was the only reason that an owl would have his own set of claws. All the claws in the Great Tree were kept in the armory. There weren't many rules at Ga'Hoole, but it was strictly forbidden to keep arms in your hollow.

But Soren was drawn to them nonetheless. Slowly, he flew in short hops toward the claws on the wall. "Well, they're rusty," Gylfie said, looking nervously at her friend. She knew how much Soren admired Ezylryb. She knew this must be difficult for him. Hireclaws were the lowest of the low.

"Because they're rusty, I don't think he uses them much. Maybe not for years and years, Soren."

"Maybe," Soren said weakly. He peered more closely at the claws. There was something familiar about them. Something in the way the claws curved in such an exact likeness to the way an owl's talons curved and were angled. *The fit must be perfect*, Soren thought. Then it burst upon him.

"Gylfie," he turned suddenly to the Elf Owl, "these claws were made by the rogue smith of Silverveil."

"No, young'uns," the two owls whirled around. Slithering into the chamber was Octavia. "Not the smith of Silverveil, but her master from Dark Fowl Island in the Everwinter Sea. They were made for Lyze of Kiel, poet, warrior, and writer of sagas."

"Lyze of Kiel," Soren whispered the words. They rang in his ears. The letters rearranged themselves in his mind's eye. Their true meaning turned in the deepest part of his gizzard.

The old blind snake seemed to sense all this. "Yes, Soren. You're getting the picture, aren't you?"

"Huh?" Gylfie said.

"Lyze of Kiel, Gylfie. Rearrange some of letters and it spells Ezyl."

CHAPTER THIRTEEN

Octavia Speaks

Yes, my dear, the 'ryb' was added after we arrived here and the owls knew that the greatest of scholars and warriors had come to the Great Ga'Hoole Tree." She paused. "You know him as Ezylryb."

At that moment, Digger entered the secret chamber. He was frantic. "I called and called trying to warn you. I tried everything to distract her. I'm really sorry."

Octavia swung her head toward the Burrowing Owl. "Don't worry. For a long time I have felt that Soren was up to something. Since that first night of the harvest festivities. I would have found out sooner or later."

Soren remembered now how Octavia had slithered out onto the gallery to help Madame Plonk, who had passed out from the milkberry wine. Everyone else had been distracted by the comet's appearance. It was the perfect distraction, camouflage for their leaving. But just as Soren was sweeping from the Great Hollow, he had felt the gaze of the sightless snake boring into him. She did have extraordinary powers, even if she had not been born blind.

"You won't tell anybody, will you, Octavia?" There was almost a pleading tone in Soren's voice.

"No. What good would that do? It wouldn't help get Ezylryb back."

"Do you think that his disappearance has something to do with his past — with someone who wants to get even?"

Octavia coiled up and extended her head directly toward Soren. He had that same feeling again as if her gaze were penetrating his deepest thoughts. "Who told you that?"

"The rogue smith."

"Of Silverveil?" Octavia lifted her head slightly. "Yes, I might have known. She's quite different from her sister, isn't she?" It was useless asking this snake how she knew anything — she just seemed to know.

But how come she doesn't know where Ezylryb is? Soren asked himself.

Now Octavia picked up her feather duster and began whisking the film of dust off a stack of books on a desk near the claws. Gylfie gave a little sneeze. "Allergies, don't worry. Go ahead, Octavia."

"The place is a mess, isn't it? It's hard for me to come in here and tidy up. Too many memories."

"Of course," Soren said softly, but he had a feeling that Octavia was about to recount some of those memories, and perhaps moving about, keeping busy with this simple task of dusting, would loosen her forked tongue.

"You see, young'uns," Octavia began as she neatened a stack of papers and continued dusting Ezylryb's desk. "Ezylryb and I go way back, back to the time when he was known as Lyze, the almost legendary warrior of the War of the Ice Claws."

The three young owls hardly dared to breathe as the chubby old snake began her tale.

"This War of the Ice Claws was the longest in history. It was well into its second century by the time Lyze was hatched. He was groomed, trained, raised to be a warrior, as were all the young owls from the Stormfast Island in the Bay of Kiel in the Everwinter Sea. His father, his mother, his grandparents, his great- and great-great-grandparents all were superb soldiers. Every single one of them had been a commander of an air artillery division. They were learned, too. Knew how to fight with their minds, not just with their talons. But it was soon apparent, as soon as Lyze first fledged and took to the wing, that this was one extraordinary young Whiskered Screech Owl. More brilliant than any of his siblings, which was later to cause trouble in the nest. He soon became the youngest commander of an air artillery division and shortly thereafter began in earnest to train colliers.

"Now you are probably wondering where I came in. Well, on the island of Stormfast there were, of course, nest-maid snakes. They were blind. But there was another breed of snake called Kielians, and they were not blind. They didn't have rosy scales, but the blue-green ones like my own. I am a Kielian snake. We are known for our industry and wit. More muscular than the blind snakes and extremely supple."

Octavia paused for a moment. "This isn't all fat, you know!" She twisted her head about and patted her body with it. "Lots of muscle there. In any case, we could get into places that were unreachable to blind snakes and, because of our musculature, we could actually dig holes, be it on the ground or in a tree. Yes, our fangs were as effective as a woodpecker's beak."

The three owls froze as two long fangs shot from her mouth.

"Scary, aren't they?" She paused to give the owls another good look, then continued with her story. "It was Lyze who first thought of using us in battle. Lyze and I were about the same age. My parents knew his parents, but there really wasn't much mingling between snakes and owls in general on Stormfast. You have to understand that creatures who live in the Everwinter Sea and along its coast aren't really sociable types. They stick to themselves. It's such a harsh environment that it, well, does not lend itself to — how should I put it? — frivolity. Except for yours truly here.

"I was a problem snake. A problem as a young'un, and it only grew worse as I grew older. I loved fooling about, having fun, getting into trouble. I don't mind telling you I was a terrible flirt in those days. It seems the whole industry thing for which our species was known had just passed me by. I can remember my mum saying once that if she didn't know better, she'd think she and Pa were raising a chipmunk. Chipmunks are silly, incredibly irresponsible, frivolous creatures. I was driving my parents to distraction by the time I was a teenager. It was just around that time that Lyze came up with the idea to train Kielian snakes for battle. One day when Lyze was flying over the rocky crag where my parents had their nest, one of the few sunny days and I was out sunning myself, doing nothing, and my mum was ranting at me. Lyze heard her from above. He had just had the idea for a stealth force of Kielian snakes. He lighted down and said to my mum, 'Give her to me, ma'am, and she'll never have another lazy day in her life. I'll turn her into a crack soldier.' I, of course, was horrified by the idea. But before I knew what had happened, Mum and Pa had nodded their consent, and I was in Lyze's talons being flown off to a training camp. The only compensation was that there were some handsome male Kielians. But my goodness, after a day's training I wasn't fit for anything but sleep.

"Well, you might not believe it, but I turned into a pretty fair soldier for the stealth force. I think it was Lyze who made me, to tell you the truth. That owl could inspire anybody."

Soren felt a twinge in his gizzard. *How true it is*, he thought, and remembered his times flying with Ezylryb through forest fires, gales, and the worst of storms.

"Lyze took a mate shortly after I came into training. In a sense, that was when his troubles with his brother really began. His brother, a seemingly quiet, gentle owl named Ifghar, had fancied Lyze's mate, but she did not fancy him. The War of the Ice Claws was getting fiercer. The league of Kiel, for it was the islands of the Bay of Kiel and the coast that had gathered into an alliance, was being beaten back by the league of the Ice Talons farther to the east. The King of the Ice Talons region was a brutal old Snowy who really wanted dominion over the entire Northern Kingdoms. It was at about that time that I was promoted to the most elite of the stealth-force units. This unit, called Glauxspeed, was in Lyze's division, of which he was the commander in chief. I served him directly.

"Lyze and his mate, Lil, made a beautiful couple in battle. It was as if they did not even have to speak. Their gizzards were so in tune, so harmonious, that they instantly knew what the other was thinking. Together, they were a fearsome team. Their timing, their precision, couldn't be matched. They were the anathema of the enemy. Everyone knew if the war was going to be won it would be because of Lyze and Lil."

"So what happened?" Digger asked. "Was the war won?"

Octavia sighed deeply and put down her duster. "No, Ifghar became a turnfeather, betrayed them, betrayed his brother, his family, the entire Kielian league. So jealous was he that, by this point, he went to the other side and swore he could break up the team. His only condition was that Lil be given to him as a mate."

"Oh, no!" all three owls said at once.

"I found out about the plan but it was too late. They were already on the wing, set to attack a recon unit on an island in the Bay of Fangs. I usually flew aboard a heavy old Barred Owl. He was a terrific flier, fast and silent, but he wasn't available. They got me a Spotted Owl instead but she didn't have the speed. I got there just in time to see the ambush led by Ifghar. It was all going according to his evil plan, except for one thing — Lil was mortally wounded. Ifghar went berserk, and Lyze . . . well, Lyze went yeep."

"Yeep!" Soren was stunned. When birds went yeep due to some enormous fright, some gizzard-chilling terror, their wings folded under and they plummeted to earth. "It was lucky that a bald eagle was flying over just then. The eagle took a plunge and caught Lyze just before he would have hit the water. But he caught him by a talon, severely injuring it. Still, it would have been worse if he had fallen into the sea. He would have drowned. Owls can't swim worth racdrops. The injured talon never healed properly. It was causing him a great deal of pain. So he finally bit it off himself."

"Bit off his own talon?" Soren said in dismay.

"Believe me, after the first pain he began feeling much better." She stopped talking.

Digger sensed that there was still more to tell. He stepped forward. "Is there something else?"

"Yes, it was in that battle — the Battle of the Ice Talons, it was later named — that I was blinded. I was so distracted with Lyze going yeep that I didn't see the fierce old Great Gray Owl coming up on the windward flank. I had coiled up to my tallest height and was frantically yelling at

Lyze to break the yeep spell. The Great Gray swept by and in two seconds plucked out my eyes. That was the end of my military career. And it turned out to be the end of Lyze's as well. He never picked up a pair of battle claws again." She paused. "Not to fight, at least." She nodded at the ones on the wall. "These old rusty ones are the ones he wore in that battle. I convinced him to retrieve them so they wouldn't fall into enemy talons."

"So what did you do?"

"Well, Lyze and I had become quite fond of each other by this time. He said that he was finished with war and had decided to retreat to a small island far from the Ice Claw Wars, which was in the Bitter Sea. There was a retreat there, an order of Glauxian brothers who were devoted only to study. They had a great library. So that is where we went for a good long time. Nobody asked any questions. Lyze read and read and read. And began his history, the one you saw on the history of the War of the Ice Claws. He also began his serious study of weather at the retreat. It was there I learned how to be a nest-maid snake and tend to his hollow and the hollows of many of the other brothers."

"Where did Madame Plonk's sister come into all this?" Gylfie asked.

"Oh, a year or so before the great tragedy, she had left her family's hollow, desperate to escape because of her stepmother. Her life was utterly miserable. Music was not for her. There was something about her that Lyze and his mate, Lil, took a fancy to. I think they liked her toughness, and she seemed extraordinarily skillful with her talons. So Lyze gave her an introduction to the rogue smith on the island of Dark Fowl."

"When did you decide to come to the great tree?"

"It was actually one of the Glauxian brothers' ideas. He felt that Lyze had so much knowledge that it was a shame for it to be all locked up in a retreat. There were no young ones at the retreat. He felt that Lyze could be a natural teacher. So he advised him to go to the Great Ga'Hoole Tree where there were always young owls to teach. And Lyze said he would but he would never ever train an owl to fight. He would never ever touch a pair of battle claws again. So we came here. I swore an oath of peace, as well." Octavia paused for several long seconds. "But you know, now I think it is time to break it. I'll do anything to rescue my beloved master."

CHAPTER FOURTEEN

Eglantine's Dream

There was stunned silence when Octavia finished her extraordinary tale. It was almost too much to absorb. Soren, Digger, and Gylfie made their way back to their hollow. It was past First Black, and Twilight and Eglantine had overslept. They were just now getting ready for evening chaw practice.

"Where have you been?" Twilight asked suspiciously.

"No time to explain now," Gylfie replied.

"We'll tell you all about it later," Soren said and turned to look at Eglantine. She looked a bit peaked. Her usually lustrous black eyes seemed dull. "You all right, Eglantine?" he asked.

"I didn't sleep that well. Bad dreams I think, but I can't remember them really."

The five owls left for their various classes. All the owls were required to attend all classes, even if they were not a member of that particular chaw. Tonight, however, they were all quite distracted and in navigation; Soren nearly crashed into Primrose.

"Soren, attention please!" Strix Struma hooted. "Too much harvest celebration, I think!" And she made a clicking sound with her beak.

In the dining hollow, near dawn after classes ended, Soren, Gylfie, Digger, Twilight, Primrose, and Eglantine gathered at Mrs. P.'s table.

"I'll stretch myself out longer," Mrs. Plithiver said, "if you'd like to invite some friends over."

"Oh, that's all right, Mrs. Plithiver," Gylfie replied. "We're fine just the six of us."

But they weren't really fine. Gylfie, Soren, and Digger were very quiet. Eglantine was twitchy; Twilight sensed that he had missed out on something important, and so did Primrose, for that matter. Soren thought it might have been better if they had invited a few other owls over, even Otulissa. A nonstop talker like Otulissa would have made it easier. Their breaklight, as this meal was often called, was delicious with Ga'Hoole nut porridge and milkberry syrup poured over it from the new harvest. Toasted mice and caterpillars dipped in a sweet juice made from the plump berries. No one, however, seemed especially hungry. In fact, they were ready to turn in by the time the first rays of the sun slid over the horizon. But first, of course, they had to go and bury pellets for Dewlap. There was only one more day and then they would have completed their flint mop. It couldn't come quickly enough.

Soon they were all asleep in the hollow. But Soren, even in his sleep, could sense his sister's restlessness as she fluttered in some storm-tossed sea of dreams. Then toward noon when the sun was reaching its highest point, a terrible shrill scream split the air of the hollow. A small tornado of downy feathers swirled up from the dreaming Eglantine.

Soren was immediately by her side. "It's just a bad dream, Eglantine, a bad dream. You're here at the tree safe in the hollow with me and Twilight and Digger and Gylfie. You're perfectly safe."

Eglantine put her talon out to touch Soren as if to make sure he was real and this was not a dream. "Soren," she spoke in a quavering voice. "I knew those stone walls that you described, where the rogue smith had her forge, reminded me of something."

"Yes?" Soren said slowly.

"Remember the isinglass when Trader Mags came last summer? When I saw that, it reminded me of something, too. It was after that, that I came out of my, my . . ."

"Condition," Gylfie added slowly.

"Yes, Gylfie. It was after that, that I recognized Soren again. Well, in this dream, I dreamed of stone, and it has helped me remember more."

"Remember what?" Soren said in a whisper. All the owls waited tensely.

"I know where they kept us now, kept all of us from the Great Downing."

"Where?" Soren was now in a fever. For months, Boron and Barran had tried to figure out the mystery of the Great Downing. Where had the owls been before? Why they had been dropped in an open field far from any hollows or nests? The owls themselves were so confused and stunned, they could give no clues as to the answers to any of their questions. In fact, for the first several days, the only words they uttered in their strange little singsongy voices were weird chants about the purity of Tytos. The owls rescued in the Great Downing had all been some sort of Barn Owl, and the formal name for the family of Barn Owls was Tytonidae, or Tytos for short. Even when they finally were rested and brought back to health, not one of them could recall what had happened to them.

Eglantine opened her beak slightly as if she were about to speak then shut her eyes tightly. There was a long pause. "You see, it comes in patches. When I saw that thin sliver of colored stone last summer — the isinglass — and the moonlight through it, and I heard the harp tuning up, I remembered how much they hated music."

"They? Who is they?" Twilight leaned forward, towering over Eglantine.

"Well, they were Barn Owls like us for the most part — some Sooties and some Grass Owls, a few Masked ones."

"Yes," Soren said slowly. "Now try and tell us more, Eglantine."

"Well, they hated music. Music was forbidden."

"Why was that?"

"I'm not sure, but for some reason we all craved music. They said we weren't working out."

"What did they mean by that?" Gylfie asked.

"I don't know." Eglantine cocked her head quickly in one direction and then the other, in the way young owls often did when they were confused or disturbed.

"Do you remember anything about the place you were in or how you got there?" Soren pressed.

"Not really."

"Was it a forest? " Digger asked.

"No. "

"Was it a deep stone pit?" said Gylfie, remembering the

bleak stone prison of St. Aggie's that spread itself through rock gulches and canyons with nary a tree or a blade of grass.

"There was stone. Most definitely there was stone like the stones of the rogue smith's forge in Silverveil, all carefully carved and stacked into walls." Eglantine blinked, and blinked again as if trying to see an image, an image dim and faded and steeped in shadows.

Soren suddenly had an idea. Last summer, Eglantine had started to shake, to have her fit, and then she remembered who she was when she had seen the fragment of the isinglass on Trader Mags' cloth. Just seeing the sliver of isinglass had jolted her out of her stunned state. And then all the owls from the Downing started clamoring to hear the music, for, indeed, Madame Plonk had just started harp practice. The owls of the Great Downing had been frantic to get to the music. And it did seem to restore them.

"Gylfie." Soren turned to the little Elf Owl. "Don't you have some isinglass from Trader Mags?"

"Yes, I was going to string it into a whirlyglass, but I haven't had the time. It's almost all strung but just not hung together yet."

"May I have a piece for a minute?" Soren asked.

"Certainly," Gylfie replied.

Just as Soren was picking up a string with sparkling pieces of the mica stone, the noonday sun flared into the hollow. Eglantine turned and gasped and her eyes fastened on the bits of glass that Soren held. Slowly, the colored spots of light dappled the air and the dancing colors spread across her brother's pure white face. "You look just like the stained glass windows in the castle," Eglantine said softly.

"A castle!" the other four owls exclaimed.

"Yes," Eglantine said. "When we first got there, we thought it was so beautiful, even though it was in ruins with many of the walls down and just parts of others standing, but we soon learned." Eglantine was talking now in a dreamy voice as if she were in some kind of a trance. "It was beautiful but there was ugliness, too. They called themselves the Pure Ones and, at first, they seemed kind. They wanted to teach us to worship Tytos because they said we were the purest of the pure of all the owls, and that is why we spoke the praising songs. But it wasn't at all the way that Mum and Da used to read to us, Soren. No, not at all. I mean, you remember how Mum would try to hum a little tune and almost sing. We could not do that. They wanted nothing to do with music. They thought music was like poison." It reminded Soren of St. Aggie's, where questions were thought to be poison and the worst punishments were reserved for those who asked questions.

"But it was the one they called the High Tyto," Eglantine continued, "he was the worst. He never said much. But he was so frightening. He wore a kind of mask, and they said his beak had been torn off in a battle." Then Eglantine realized what she had just said and fell into a faint.

"Metal Beak!" they all whispered in terror.

Gylfie immediately began flying over Eglantine, wafting drafts of air down upon her face to revive her. Twilight also tried, but his wings churned the air so violently that Eglantine was practically lifted off the floor of the hollow.

Eglantine's eyes blinked open. "My goodness, I fainted, didn't I?" Then she looked up at Soren as she staggered to her feet.

"Take it easy now, little one," Twilight said. "You've just had a bad fright."

"No, no I'm fine. I'm really fine. I feel so much better. But just imagine — I came face-to-face with Metal Beak. It's all coming back to me now. He was the one who hated music the most. He thought it was impure. In fact, he thought any owl who was not a Tyto alba was a little less than completely pure. He made the Sooties and the

Masked Owls and the Grass Owls do all the worst jobs. Oh, and yes, before we could become true members of the Way of Purity, we had to sleep in stone crypts with the bones of the old Tytos that they called the Purest Ones."

"The Purest Ones?" Soren said, perplexed.

Gylfie had remained very quiet, but when she heard about the little owls being put in the stone crypts, she began to speak. "I think that they did to Eglantine with stone what the owls of St. Aggie's did to us with the full moon." Gylfie was referring to the horrendous moon-blinking process during which the young owlets at St. Aggie's were forced to sleep with their heads directly exposed to the scalding light of the moon. It disturbed their gizzards in a profound way and seemed to destroy their will, along with any of the individual characteristics that made up an owl's personality.

Gylfie continued, "Only instead of being moon blinked, they were stone stunned. I think I've heard of it. In the Desert of Kuneer, there are a series of deep, blind canyons — a maze really — and if one gets lost in them, the stone can affect the brain. If the owls come back, they are a bit odd, you know, weird in the head." But there was something else that Gylfie felt in her gizzard but did not mention. She was almost sure that the bones in those crypts were not the bones of owls, but of the Others. The thought, however, was too chilling, too sickeningly terrifying to even mention.

Soren's eyes fastened on Eglantine's wing where she had suffered her most severe wound from the Great Downing. The feathers had grown back, but patchily. He felt swollen with anger at this vile owl Metal Beak. "I can't believe how he hurt you, Eglantine. It makes me want to kill him. No wonder Mum's and Da's scrooms warned me."

"But you don't understand, Soren. It wasn't the Tyto owls of the castle that did this to my wing. Oh, they did plenty. Feelings in my gizzard are just really coming back now, but it was the other owls, the ones who raided the castle and snatched us. That is really how I and all the rest of us got hurt. They nearly got away with us but the owls from the castle, the High Tyto and the Pure Ones, followed. There was this huge battle as they tried to snatch us back, and I dropped. So did a lot of us because something came along and scared them all. I was surprised that I survived the fall. But then I was worried that I would be snatched again. That is why I dragged myself to hide under that bush where Digger and Twilight found me."

"Were the owls who snatched you, Barn Owls as well?" Gylfie asked.

"Oh, no. All sorts. There was a raggedy-looking Great Horned, and she had a huge bare patch on her wing that made her fly all funny."

"Skench!" Gylfie and Soren both blurted out at once. Skench, whose cruelty knew no bounds, the Ablah General of St. Aegolius Academy for Orphaned Owls had just such a patch on her wing.

"So they were from St. Aggie's!" Soren said.

It had all come back so clearly to Eglantine that now she could hardly stop talking. But meanwhile, one thought prevailed in Soren's mind. Were they actually any closer to finding Ezylryb? Could Eglantine remember where this castle was with its odd rituals that celebrated the purity of Barn Owls in such an awful way? Was Ezylryb there, or had he simply gotten lost? Had he been stone stunned? Or was he dead?

CHAPTER FIFTEEN
The Chaw of Chaws

In times of trouble, however, there can come a certain closeness, a kind of coziness of spirit. It was never so true as in the hollow of Soren and his mates, Gylfie, Twilight, Digger, and now Eglantine. The stories that Eglantine told held a peculiar fascination for the owls in the hollow. Finally, it was Digger who asked, "Eglantine, can you remember what the ground was like around the castle? I mean, was it like Silverveil or The Beaks?"

"I've never been to The Beaks, but how do you mean, Digger?"

"Well, were there tall trees, or was it scrubby with short bushy plants? Was it hard-packed earth, bare, or maybe sandy like a desert?"

"Oh, none of those, I think. I can't remember exactly, for they hardly ever let us out. Although from the broken walls, I could catch a glimpse. They didn't permit us to fly up high. I think there was grass, though. And they used to speak of a meadow. But I don't think there were big trees or trees with leaves, because I can remember when I was just hatched, the hollow in our fir tree — remember, Soren, how you could hear the wind through the leaves of the nearby trees? No, we only heard the wind whistling around the stone corners of the castle."

"Well, that's helpful," Digger said thoughtfully.

"Why?" asked Gylfie.

"I was just thinking, that's all." There was a tense silence in the hollow.

But Soren was thinking, too. Of course, Digger would be interested in the ground. Digger knew the ground — what kind of plants grew there, the feeling of every kind of soil. He had become one of the best in the tracking chaw. In fact, when Soren gazed around he realized that within this hollow were the best of the best of each chaw.

"Eglantine," Soren asked, "do you remember how long you had been flying before you were dropped?"

"Not long, I think." There was another pause.

"Eglantine, do you think that there is any way you might be able to lead us back to the castle? You see, I am thinking that it's been more than two months since Ezyl-ryb disappeared. Endless search parties have been sent out but so far nothing. In fact, Boron just assumed that was what we were doing when we went to Silverveil. Indirectly it was, but really we went to find out more about Metal Beak. Now, what's to stop us from trying to find Ezylryb? Between us . . ." Soren stopped and looked around. "We could put together a pretty good chaw."

"What are you talking about, Soren?" Gylfie asked.

"Gylfie, you are the best navigator Strix Struma has ever taught. I heard her telling that to Barran. Digger, you can track like no one else, and Twilight you can fight" — Soren's voice dropped off — "if that's necessary." Twilight swelled in anticipation. "Don't you see?" Soren continued. "We have the makings here of a great chaw — the best of the best of the chaws."

"Let me get this straight," Gylfie said. The little Elf Owl stepped right up to Soren and stood directly under his beak. "Are you proposing that we should undertake this search for Ezylryb on our own? No rybs, no grown-up owls?"

"That's exactly what he's proposing, Gylfie," Twilight boomed. "For Glaux's sake, we went to Silverveil on our own. Found the rogue smith. She gave us our first real clue, in a sense, about Metal Beak." Twilight paused and nodded deferentially to Soren. "Well, after the scrooms of your mum and da that is."

"Well, if that is the case . . ." Gylfie's voice fell to a whisper. Soren was nervous. If he didn't have Gylfie's support, he couldn't do it. "If that is the case, Soren, you must be our leader."

All of the owls in the hollow nodded their heads in agreement. Soren was stunned. He didn't know what to say. Finally, he spoke. "I thought the plan up, that is true. But the plan would be nothing without each one of you. Your faith in me has stirred my gizzard. I shall do my best for you."

"Soren!" Otulissa suddenly flew into the hollow. "I want to come, too." The meddlesome Spotted Owl had been perched on a branch just outside the hollow. Otulissa's yellow eyes were dim with tears. "Ezylryb made me believe in myself and not just my . . . my . . ." It was the first time Otulissa had ever been at a loss for words. "You know how I was before I joined the chaw. Ezylryb made me believe I could do things because I was just me, and not just because I was a Spotted Owl. I hate that thing that you were talking about before."

"What thing?" Soren asked.

"That stuff about purity, that one kind of owl is more pure or better than another. The most ancient order of owls, the owls that all of us are descended from — whether we are Barn Owls, Snowies, Spotted, or whatever — those first owls were all called Glaux. And every owl celebrates the spirit of Glaux. My mum told me that, and it is true. For indeed with that ancient order began a special kind of bird. As owls, we owe our uniqueness, our ability to fly silently, to see through the darkness of the night, to spin our heads almost all the way around to those first owls. And you know from navigation that we call our grandest constellation that shines through every season the Great Glaux. But for those owls that Eglantine talked about, that was not enough. They want to destroy all the others."

They were all dismayed by Otulissa's gracious speech. Soren thought that she must have been eavesdropping more than once to have learned all this. She almost started to blubber now with tears and chokes. It was the most un-Otulissa moment any of them had ever witnessed. "I feel so strongly about this. You know me, I'm not an emotional kind of owl but this . . . this . . . I . . . I can't explain, but you must let me be a part of this."

"Of course," Soren said. Otulissa was very smart and beyond being smart, she of all of them possessed the most sensitivity to atmospheric pressure changes. She had proved herself invaluable to the weather chaw.

And this would be the best of the best of the chaws! Indeed, it would be the chaw of chaws!

CHAPTER SIXTEEN

The Empty Shrine

They had picked an evening to leave when there were no classes and no chaw practices, but still they were careful to leave the tree in twos or threes near First Black and then once again take off from the cliffs where they would not be spotted. And they all, even the smallest, wore battle claws. They had filched them from the armory in the forge. Bubo happened to be gone so it was not a problem. Twilight had gone early in the morning of their flight and taken them from the forge and placed them in the crags of the cliffs.

Soren had insisted that they practice with the claws, for none of them had flown that often with them. Eglantine had never flown "clawed," as the expression went.

"You need a lot of tail ruddering, Eglantine. See, you don't have the same balance as before," Soren called out as he watched his sister fly in a wobbly line out from the cliffs.

"She'll get it," Twilight said.

But Soren wasn't sure. Eglantine still seemed so fragile to him. Was she ready for this? She was the only one who would be able to recognize the ruined castle where she had been imprisoned. But then suddenly her flight seemed to even out.

"That's it! That's it!" Soren cheered her on, her wings set and balanced on a smooth horizontal plane. "Phew!" Soren blew through his beak in relief. Still, it disturbed him that he was in fact doing just the opposite of what Ezylryb had sworn never to do again. Soren was not only picking up battle claws but arming a young innocent owl with them, as well. Then he thought of Octavia and the words she had spoken to them in the very chamber where Ezylryb's old claws hung rusted but not forgotten. *I swore an oath of peace, as well. But you know, now I think it is time to break it. I'll do anything to rescue my beloved master.*

The time had come, Soren realized. If there was any chance of rescuing Ezylryb they must do it now before winter set in. There was no choice. The first blizzard could happen any day now and by then it might be too late. Soren ordered Eglantine back to the cliff. Then he stood before the chaw and spoke in a quiet but strong voice that did not waver as he gave the order. "Flight positions. Get ready to fly. Lift!"

And six owls rose into the night.

The plan was to first fly back to the place where Eglantine had been found in the Forest Kingdom of Ambala. They would then somehow try, with Eglantine's help, to find their way to the castle ruins and hopefully to Ezylryb. As they flew, Soren wondered that if they were successful in reaching the castle, and if Ezylryb was there, how would they actually rescue him? Perhaps he shouldn't think so far in advance. When they got there, maybe a plan would come to him. The first task was to get there — to this awful place where young owls were forced to sleep in crypts with bones of these so-called Purest Ones, whatever that really meant.

Twilight was flying point at the moment and Digger flying below, for they were the ones who knew the territory where Eglantine had been found. "We are in Ambala and approaching the area of the Great Downing," Twilight called down to Digger. Digger immediately went into a ground dive. Gylfie began to hover over him.

Twilight turned to Soren and nodded. This was the place. Soren looked up and found the Star That Never Moves.

"Gylfie, take a sighting of our position between Never Moves and the first head star of the Great Glaux constellation."

When Gylfie had their position fixed, they all began to spiral down, except Twilight. Twilight continued to hover above — alert for any other owls in the region. Then, with Digger and the others, they would try to work backward from the spot where Eglantine had been found and reconstruct a path to the castle ruins.

They lighted down in the dry creek bed. "Well, the tracks are gone by now as I expected," Digger said. "But I do remember where I first picked them up."

"Let's start with the actual bush where you first found her, Digger."

With long strides, the Burrowing Owl was there in no time. The others followed.

"Oh, my!" said Eglantine. "This is surely the place. I wouldn't forget it. It seemed as if I spent forever here."

"Now, Eglantine," Digger said, "fly along this creek bed and try to remember where you were dropped."

They had flown less than a minute. "Do you think it was here?" Digger asked. For this was where he had picked up her tracks.

"No, I think it was farther. It was pretty wet."

They flew a few more minutes. "Here! Here!" Eglantine

suddenly said. She lighted down. There was a very small, gurgling stream of water, no more than a few inches deep. "I remember that rock!" She lifted a talon and pointed. "I remember thinking, 'Lucky I didn't fall on that.'"

"Good! Good!" said Soren. "Prepare to fly! We'll make at least three circles overhead and, Eglantine, you try and sense which direction you came from."

"Oh, I don't know, Soren. That's going to be hard. I was so scared, and there was so much commotion. I mean, it was a battle up there."

"Just do your best, Eglantine. That's all you can do. If we have to, we'll fly out in every direction from this spot — Gylfie, you're navigator, so keep track of our position."

Eglantine couldn't remember, and they did begin the slow process of flying out in all directions.

The night is not simply black to an owl. There are layers of blackness of different densities. Sometimes the black is thick, a gooey black unleavened by starlight or the moon, and sometimes the black is thin — still black, but an almost transparent sort of blackness. It all has to do with the shine and the set of the moon above, of the constellations rising or vanishing, and the features of the earth below — whether the land is clad in forests or barren and hard with rock. Just as Twilight was an expert at seeing through the very deceptive grays of twilight and dawn, so Soren was skillful in "reading the black" of the full night.

"Thin-to-coarse black," he called out as they flew over a sparsely wooded area. Then, half an hour later as they flew in another direction, "Water black turning to crunchy."

"No!" said Eglantine, "I know that we never flew over water."

The owls banked steeply and went back to their starting positions. As they settled down on the limbs of a tree, Gylfie suddenly had a brilliant thought. "If these owls just wanted Barn Owls, and mostly Tyto albas, at that, doesn't it make sense that their castle might be located either in Tyto or very near one of its boundaries? More specifically, the boundary it shares with Ambala, which is very small."

So they headed in the direction of the Ambala-Tyto boundary. Soren asked Otulissa to fly out as a scout. It was not long before she came back with the report of a meadow. "Upwind and to the west, but I spotted a forest fire just a little bit north of west. I would say two points off the second head star of the Great Glaux. I don't think we need to worry with the wind in this direction."

"Good work, Otulissa," Soren said.

*   *   *

Soon the walls of the castle ruins rose in the dawn mist. Only one tower had remained complete. The rest had crumbled down, so they stood only slightly higher than the castle walls. A peaceful haze rolled over the meadow below.

"We'd better fetch up in that small grove of trees," Soren said. "I have a feeling there might be crows around."

From their perches in an alder, the six owls had a good view of the castle. It must have been lovely in its time, Soren imagined, and even in its ruined state, two stained glass windows could be seen in the still-standing east wall. An embroidery of ivy and moss crept over the stone.

"It seems different," Eglantine said after several minutes.

"How?" asked Soren

"Well, it seems very still."

"But it's almost full morning. They are all probably asleep."

"I know, but at full morning the guard usually changes. That's why I said we had to get here just before dawn — exactly at twixt time. The tower has no view toward the east and, at twixt time, the guard changes so we are really safe. But I would be able to see the changing of the guard, for the old guard usually circles the tower one time upon leaving."

"I haven't seen any owls circling," said Twilight.

"And the hunters usually went out to catch a few meadow voles. It's a good time just after twixt time for catching them," Eglantine added.

They waited a good while longer. Finally, Eglantine sighed. "I think something is very odd. It is just too still. Look — see that deer going up to the east wall? That would never happen if the owls were there. . . . But I wouldn't want to be wrong. I mean, I wouldn't want us to go in there and then be attacked."

Soren had been thinking the same thing. He had an idea. "Gylfie, do you think you could fly through that meadow grass without getting tangled up and have a closer look?"

She gave him a shocked look. "Of course. Look, Soren, with all due respect, I might be a noisy flier compared to some but I can thread my way through that grass like a nest-maid through harp strings." Elf and Pygmy Owls, although quite small, were considered noisy fliers for they lacked the soft fringe feathers known as plummels that swallowed the sound of their wings passing through the air.

"Good. I was never doubting your abilities, really. Now, why don't you go up and take a look? But be careful. Come back at the first sign of any danger."

Gylfie was off before they could wish her well.

"Great Glaux," Otulissa sighed. "Look at her go. She might be noisy but look, the grass is hardly moving where she flies through."

Gylfie was back in less than a quarter of an hour. "It's empty. Completely empty."

"No sign, I take it, of Ezylryb?" Soren asked.

"Not that I could see."

"Well, we better have a look for ourselves, then." Soren paused a moment and gazed toward the castle. "All right. We'd all better go together in a tight formation in case of crows. At the first sign of crows, we'll all pack in tight. There are six of us. I can't believe they'd mob us."

A thrush whistled softly in a gallery as the owls lighted down within the cool shadows of the highest wall of the castle ruins. There were things in this place that Soren had never seen before, things that were not of the forest or the meadows or the deserts or the canyons. An immense gilded — but rotting — thing that Eglantine called a throne, where she said the High Tyto perched. There were stumps of broken stone columns with grooves carved in them. "What is that?" asked Soren, pointing with his talon to a high stone perch with stone ledges leading up to it.

"Well," said Eglantine hesitantly, "it was from there that the High Tyto often spoke to us when he was not perched on the throne."

"The High Tyto?" Soren asked. "You mean Metal Beak?"

"Yes. Sometimes they called him 'His Pureness,' but never Metal Beak."

"Great Glaux, it makes me want to yarp!" Twilight snarled. "This purity stuff sounds deadly."

Soren thought that perhaps Twilight didn't realize how true his words really were.

"But I know no one is here," Eglantine continued. "Because of that thrush in the gallery. No one was ever allowed up there."

Eglantine stood quietly peering one way and then the other. It was hard for her to believe that she was back here, but back now with her dear brother, which was even stranger.

She sometimes wondered about Kludd. But she had a bad feeling about him. She had a feeling that he might have had something to do with her fall, as he had with Soren's. She was never absolutely sure. By the time she fell, he was flying about all over, even when he was supposed to be in the nest with her when their parents were out hunting. He made her swear that she would never tell that he'd left her. One night, he came back with blood all over him. She had no idea where he had been, but when their parents came back he told a lie. He said that a fox had been scuttling around at the bottom of the fir tree, and he thought he could get it. Their father was furious. "You could have gotten yourself killed, Kludd."

"Well, it was just a small fox. I wanted to do something nice for you and Mum."

It was a complete lie.

"What's this?" Gylfie said. She was perched in a wooden niche.

Eglantine gulped. "The shrine. That's what they called it, but it's empty!"

Gylfie cocked her head to one side then the other. Then she flipped it back so her beak almost touched the feathers between her shoulders. "It sure is!"

"And they're gone!"

"What's gone?" Soren asked. It was clear that Eglantine was very agitated.

"The Sacred Flecks of the Shrine Most Pure."

"Flecks!" Soren and Gylfie gasped in horror. Flecks — like the ones at St. Aggie's!

CHAPTER SEVENTEEN

A Muddled Owl

In a large spruce tree, the old Whiskered Screech Owl wrapped his seven talons tightly around a slender branch. His head was so muddled it was all he could do to concentrate enough to stay on the limb. He was completely disoriented and had been since he had flown across the small river at the edge of the Kingdom of Tyto. He could have sworn he was flying north, but then none of the stars seemed to line up properly. The Golden Talons, so beautiful this time of year, appeared to him upside down in the sky. And when he thought he was banking for an easterly turn, instead of flying into the glimmer of a rising sun at dawn, he was flying into the darkness of the west. He had known he might be going yoicks when for a trace of a second he thought, well, maybe the sun does rise in the west. And then he realized he had been flying around in circles for days. Finally exhausted, he had settled on the branch of a spruce, so confused he could hardly hunt. Luckily, the food supply seemed plentiful or

he would have starved. But summer had passed into autumn and soon autumn would be chased away by the first
bitter winds of winter. He would starve, he supposed. *One
can never plan these things*, he thought. He had always imagined he would get snuffed into a hurricane's eye and spin
around until he died or be sucked up by a rogue tornado
wind — the kind they called a torque demon — that tore
across the landscape and could pull up not just one tree or
two but an entire forest. There was even a story that one
torque demon had sucked up a raging forest fire and
dumped it on another forest, igniting it as well. Ezylryb
snorted. *A fitting end for an old weather owl like me.*

Every day, and he was not even sure how many days
had passed now, but with each day he grew more and
more confused. Soon, he imagined he would be too confused to even hunt in the very small area that he was able
to manage now. So this was what it had all come to. This
was to be his death. He shivered as a cool autumn breeze
with more than a hint of winter in it ruffled his feathers.
He tried to be philosophical about it. He had, indeed, led
a grand life — full of adventure, books, and young owls to
teach — scholar, sports owl, lover of a dirty joke or two.
There had been danger, yes, and heartbreak. He closed his
eyes and a tear squeezed out as he thought of his dear Lil.
But he had tried to serve well. He hoped, nobly. *Now,* he

thought, *in the deep winter of my life, I am on the brink of another winter, my last.*

Ezylryb tried to imagine what he would miss the most. Perhaps the peace of the dawn, the moment of twixt time that hung like a sparkling jewel between the gray of the night and the pink of a new morning. The young'uns — yes, undoubtedly, the young owls whom, throughout the years, he had brought into his chaw and taught to be fair navigators through any weather. Weather, he did like weather. He supposed that was what he did not like about this particular end. It wasn't a torque demon, and it wasn't the eye of a hurricane. It was in fact rather humiliating to die teetering and confused in a forest that he had thought he knew so well.

CHAPTER EIGHTEEN
A Nightmare Revisited

That horrid old St. Aggie's song began to worm its way into Soren's and Gylfie's brains.

> We shall dissect every pellet with glee.
> Perhaps we shall find a rodent's knee.
> And never will we tire
> in the sacred task that we conspire.
> Nor do our work less than perfectly
> and those bright flecks at the core,
> which make our hearts soar,
> shall always remain a mystery . . .

This was the song that Soren and Gylfie had been forced to sing as they worked in the pelletorium of St. Aggie's. Now it began to roar silently in their heads as they stood in the ruins of the castle and looked up at the empty shrine. Eglantine's dreadful words, "the sacred flecks," still rang in their ears.

"The flecks!" Soren and Gylfie both exclaimed again and stared at each other. The other owls were silent. Finally, the mystery of the flecks, which they had never unraveled, had begun to reveal itself. The image of Skench storming into the library in full battle regalia came back to them in all its terror. They had been just about to fly out of the library, the highest point in the stone maze of St. Aggie's, which offered the best escape route, and Skench, twice their size, advanced toward them, battle claws extended, a fearsome, horrific figure. And then suddenly, for no explainable reason, she slammed into the wall, drawn by some incredible force, and was rendered helpless. Thus, they had escaped. Now Soren remembered one of his very first conversations with Bubo as to why the blacksmith was "drawn to live in a cave." Bubo's words came back to him: *It be a strange and most peculiar force. It's as if all these years working with the iron, we get a bit of the magnet in us. Like them special metals — you know, iron. It's got what we call a "field." Well, you'll be learning this in metals class, in higher magnetics, where all the unseeable parts are lined up. It makes this force that draws you — same thing with me — I get drawn to the very earth from which them little flecks of iron come from.*

Now, finally, Soren realized what the force was.

"The flecks were stored in that wall in the library," Gylfie said.

"Yes, and Skench was wearing metal. There was a strange interaction. But she was so stupid, she didn't know," Soren replied.

"It's simple," said Otulissa.

"Simple?" Digger asked.

"It's higher magnetics. The second volume of Strix Emerilla focuses on disturbances and abnormalities in the earth's magnetic fields. The St. Aggie's owls might not have known what they were doing with flecks but, believe me, these owls of the castle know exactly what they are doing." Otulissa paused dramatically.

What are they doing? The question hung silently in the air.

"Should I go on?" Otulissa asked. She was clearly relishing her superior knowledge.

"Oh, for Glaux's sake, yes!" roared Twilight, seeming to swell to twice his size.

So Otulissa explained how an owl's brain could become muddled to the point of complete directional confusion so that it would be impossible for him to navigate. She was talking on and on, becoming increasingly technical, when Soren finally interrupted. "Eglantine, how many sacred flecks were there?"

"Three golden bags full."

"How big were the bags?"

She thought a moment. "Oh, about the size of" — she hesitated — "an owl's head, say, a Great Gray." She looked at Twilight.

"But how, if the sacred flecks were kept in this shrine, as you call it, how did the owls here protect themselves against the disturbances?"

"Especially Metal Beak," Gylfie added. Soren hadn't thought of this, but why wouldn't Metal Beak slam right into the bags in the same way Skench had in the library?

"I don't know," Eglantine said. "But we never felt anything." She hesitated again. "But maybe we did. When they forced us to sleep in the crypts. Sometimes I felt a strange buzzing in my head, and I would get very confused."

"Aha!" Otulissa exclaimed. She had flown up to the shrine and was investigating the doors that shuttered it closed. "Just as I suspected." She tapped her beak on the lining of the doors. "Mu!"

"Mu?" All the owls said at once.

"Mu metal — magnetically very soft. Surround a magnetic object with it, and it blocks the field. That's what protected you, Eglantine."

"Except when I was put into the crypt."

"And that is what protected Metal Beak," Gylfie said. "His mask and beak must be made of mu metal."

"Precisely," Otulissa nodded sagely.

Soren had said nothing. He was listening and thinking. "There were three bags, Eglantine, right?"

Eglantine nodded.

"But now they are gone." Soren turned toward Otulissa. "Otulissa, what would happen if you set up these three bags of flecks at certain points?"

Otulissa began to tremble, then in a barely audible whisper, she spoke. "There would be a Devil's Triangle."

"So the mu metal protects one from the magnetic disruption. But is there anything that can actually destroy the flecks, the magnetism itself forever?"

Otulissa nodded solemnly. "Fire!"

"Fire . . . mu . . . fire, fire!" Soren spread his wings and rose in flight. He swept from one corner of the castle ruins to another. It was the owl manner of pacing. To fly, to move, helped him to think. Gylfie soon lifted into flight. How often during their long imprisonment at St. Aggie's had the two of them plotted and planned together? Soren felt the comfort of Gylfie's presence as the Elf Owl fell into flight beside him. The other owls were very still except for the smooth turnings of their heads as they followed the two owls' flight with their eyes. Several minutes later, Gylfie and Soren lighted down.

"Is there any way we can get that mu off the doors of the shrine?"

"That shouldn't be hard, especially if it's soft metal," Twilight said, and flew toward the niche. Then with a force that would have torn a fox in half, he ripped off the metal.

"Good!" Soren said. "Now we must leave our battle claws behind and fly out to find that forest fire that Gylfie spotted earlier. Twilight, seeing as we have no coal-carrying buckets, could you somehow bend one of those sheets of mu metal into something like a bucket?"

"Sure thing, Soren."

Thus, a plan had been devised by Soren and Gylfie with the mu metal to protect and shield them. Since the bags were missing, it might be very easy for the owls to accidentally find themselves smack in the middle of a Devil's Triangle. As an ultimate precaution, they intended to first fly to the forest fire and collect burning coals. And, if they did fly upon the bags of sacred flecks, they could, with the coals harvested from the forest fire, destroy the flecks' power. If this triangle existed, they must destroy it. It would be a hazard to all bird life — owls, eagles, seagulls — yes, even crows — as much as they loathed that latter species. Something like this simply could not exist in nature. Otulissa thought that because she was indeed so sensitive to changes in atmospheric pressure she might be able to sense the perimeter of the triangle. So it was decided that Otulissa would fly in the point position.

They had been in the castle a long time. The light was seeping out of the day. Soon it would be First Black. The owls perched on the jagged edges of the north wall of the church and watched the smudge of smoke from an immense forest fire roll up to meet the coming darkness of the night. Gylfie stood beside Soren, hardly reaching his breast feathers. Six owls they were, Soren thought as he slid his head around to look at them. Six strong, quick-witted owls about to fulfill a destiny. They had indeed become a band of owls who would rise into the blackness and embark on the last part of a dangerous quest — to find the lost, to mend the broken, to make the world a better place, and to make each owl the best he or she could be. Soren knew that he was in fact the leader of the best of the best. And so he vowed that no matter how difficult this was, he would do all in his power to not only rescue Ezylryb, but to bring each one of these owls home safe to the Great Ga'Hoole Tree.

CHAPTER NINETEEN
Into the Devil's Triangle

It was, of course, Soren and Otulissa who, as trained colliers, would plunge into the forest fire to retrieve the coals. They had found a high rock ledge downwind of the forest fire that offered them the best point of observation. All the owls were massed on the ledge and listened carefully as Soren began to speak.

"Now, you understand that it is only myself and Otulissa who will go into the fire."

Twilight, Digger, Gylfie, and Eglantine nodded gravely. There would be no argument, not even from Twilight. They all knew that only these two owls had been trained in this very dangerous work that demanded skills far beyond the ordinary. From breathing and flying, to the beak work of seizing a live coal, these owls had received the most specialized of instruction of any chaw.

"If there is a problem, an enemy approaching or whatever — yes, come fetch us. I think it should be Gylfie or Eglantine, because Twilight and Digger, being larger, might have to remain to deal with an enemy. If either of you have to come to us, you must fly what we call the fringes of the fire."

"But what if you're not there when we come?"

"One of us will always be flying lookout, watching for the one below who is retrieving coals on the ground."

How he now wished that Ruby was here. The Short-eared Owl, being the best flier of them all, was particularly skilled in catching airborne embers. There would really be no one to fill that spot tonight. And how he missed Martin, who often performed the wide coal reconnaissance surveys that gave information as to the size and location of various rich ember beds. In addition to that, Martin was very good at finding glowworms. A glowworm was a particular kind of coal that was especially valued by Bubo for his forge. No one had the slightest idea why it was called a glowworm, but there were extra points for those who found them.

"Otulissa?" Soren said.

"Yes, Soren?"

Glaux, he hoped she didn't give him trouble. "Otulissa, you and I shall make alternating dives once we find an entry point, a good shoot. The rest of you must stay with the mu bucket once we find a place to stash it." It did not look exactly like a bucket but rather a shallow pan. It might be hard keeping the coals in it, but if they flew steady, he felt they could work with it. "Now, the good news is that we don't have to harvest nearly as many coals as we normally do. Remember, we don't need coals for a forge, but just for these three bags of flecks."

For the first time, Soren realized he had not cringed as he usually did when he said or heard the word "flecks." Perhaps this was because he was beginning to understand flecks. Yes, they had power, but at the same time, their power was not absolute. He and the band could damage this power and possibly destroy it. Soren realized suddenly that with this small bit of knowledge he had acquired in the last few hours, he knew a great deal more than the brutal owls of St. Aggie's. Whether he knew as much or more as the Pure Ones, as Eglantine had called them, and this horrendous owl called Metal Beak, remained to be seen.

A few minutes later, Soren and Otulissa were shredding the fringes of the forest fire. Shredding was a flight maneuver in which they darted in and out of what they called the dead places at the edge of the fire to find which points would be the best to actually dive in from. This was now Soren's job. Usually Elvan, the co-ryb of colliering, along with Ezylryb led the shred. But Ezylryb had insisted on Soren flying directly behind Elvan enough times that

Soren thought he could do it now. Often they had to make as many as twenty shreds before they found a point of entry. They had made four shreds so far. Now, on this fifth one, Soren felt "a shoot," or a good passageway open up.

"I think this might be it," he said to Otulissa. They made one more pass at the shoot. "All right, let's find a place nearby to stash this mu bucket and then get to work."

When they had found the place for the bucket, Soren and Otulissa left the other owls to guard it and flew toward the fire. Its roar was deafening as it gobbled the trees below. Soren fervently hoped that Eglantine would not have to come to warn them of anything. For an owl not accustomed to flying in forest fires, it was the roar rather than the heat that was often the most intimidating. And now Soren gave the command.

"DIVE!" Otulissa went into a dizzying spiral plunge. Soren kept his eye glued to her as her spots blurred. How often had he done this, flown surveillance not for Otulissa but his chaw partner, Martin? He remembered so well the first time. He had been frightened for Martin but frightened for himself as well. They had imagined every kind of horror that a forest fire could serve up. The rogue winds, the crowning when the fire in an unbridled rage would leap from treetop to treetop, creating fuel ladders that sucked up everything in their deadly heat — including owls on the wing. Yet, nothing really had scared him as much as that hurricane that had caused Martin to plummet into the sea.

Soren kept his eyes on Otulissa below as he recalled all this. He saw the Spotted Owl rising now on a stack of heated updrafts. She whirled in next to Soren, her once-creamy white spots dark with soot. A glowworm sparkled in her beak as she flew to where the mu bucket had been stashed. Now it was Soren's turn. Down he plunged. The coal beds were rich and the size of the sizzling nuggets, although smallish, burned hot. He managed to harvest two at once and flew directly back to the mu bucket.

It only took four more rounds each for Soren and Otulissa to gather enough coals. Well before midnight they turned back to the ledge where the other owls awaited them by the bucket.

Soren and Eglantine carried the mu bucket between them now with dozens of glowing coals. Twilight, being the largest and strongest of the owls, carried in his talons the piece of the mu metal, which had not been turned into a bucket, as a shield against the flecks if they should encounter any of the missing bags. Otulissa was still flying the point position.

Gylfie, the tiniest owl, flew a few feet from the ground

for close surveillance. And Digger would do what he did better than any owl — walk.

It was Otulissa's hunch that by either being very small or, indeed, walking like Digger, these two owls might be able to pass under the destructive flecks' magnetic field, if the flecks were placed high in trees. The plan was that if they found the bags of flecks they would burn them, thus destroying what Otulissa called the "magnetic alignment." It was definitely higher magnetics, and Soren was awfully glad that Otulissa had done the reading. But then again, they could do all of this and still not find any signs of Ezylryb, who might be dead for all they knew. But Soren could not even think of that, and he could not allow the other owls to think of it, either. They were on a rescue mission. Rescue was to save living creatures. And Soren had a very strong sense that somehow Ezylryb's disappearance was linked to Metal Beak. *Gizzuition*, Ezylryb had once called this sense. It was a way of knowing, a kind of thinking. Ezylryb's words came back to him: *a kind of thinking beyond the normal reasoning processes by which one immediately apprehends the truth, perceives and understands reality*. And he had said that Soren had it, that Soren possessed this strange way of knowing. How it had thrilled Soren when Ezylryb had said this, said in essence that he was special — a special owl.

* * *

"Mu shield!" Otulissa banked sharply and flew back. "I felt it. I definitely felt it."

Soren quickly commanded Gylfie and Digger, who flew and walked beneath them to proceed slowly and with great caution. Now it was Twilight who flew in the point position, holding the sheet of mu metal by his talons like a shield. The other owls flew in behind him. Every few seconds, Otulissa would tip her head out and expose herself directly to the magnetic force. If she peeked her head out to the port side of the shield, and came back blinking and looking confused, they knew they were heading in the direction of one of the bags of flecks, and they would destroy it! It seemed to them now that before they could find Ezylryb they must commit themselves to destroying the three bags of flecks that could threaten all owls' and other birds' flight and navigation abilities. If Otulissa peeked out to the starboard side and felt no change, they knew they were off course from the flecks. Gylfie and Digger flew or walked below completely undisturbed as Otulissa had thought they would.

It took them a while to navigate toward the first bag, and it was actually Digger who spotted it from the ground and called up, "Alder tree ahead. Object wedged between limb and trunk."

Protecting themselves with the shield, they flew to the

tree. Their timing was precise. Twilight passed the shield to Soren who had given the coal bucket to Eglantine. He then reached out with one talon and gave a quick push to the bag, which fell to the ground. Immediately, the effect could be seen on Gylfie and Digger. Digger began to stagger, and Gylfie simply lighted down. Her wings, in a yeep state, hung at her sides as both owls felt the strange buzz in their heads. Soren dipped his beak into the bucket and dropped the coals on the bag with perfect accuracy. There was a flare as the bag caught fire. After several minutes, Otulissa peeked out from behind the shield. "It's a miracle!" Otulissa said and stepped out from behind the shield. The magnetic force at this point had been completely destroyed. Digger and Gylfie, looking fully alert once more, picked themselves up. Digger began to walk straight again, and immediately headed toward the burning clump. He kicked up some dirt with his talons to put out the fire.

"Don't put it all out. We might need some more coals," Soren said. He retrieved some of the brightest coals from the fire, and Otulissa scooped up some cinders. The other owls watched amazed.

"How do they do it?" Digger whispered.

When the owls had the coals and were sure that the remains of the fire were safely smothered, they lifted off into flight.

They had destroyed one bag, but that was only one point of the triangle. The second point would be the hardest to discover, for it could be anywhere radiating out from this first point. They didn't know if this particular triangle was pointing east, west, north, or south. They flew almost an hour in various directions before Otulissa began to sense a disturbance. Then everything happened quickly.

"Oak!" Gylfie called up. From her low-flying position, she sensed that the disturbance that she was feeling came from the large tree dead ahead.

This time the bag of flecks was stuffed into a hollow, and because the hollow was slightly damp, they were able to burn the bag right inside, thus containing the fire and not setting the entire tree ablaze. Digger flew up with talons, grasping clots of wet mud to extinguish the flames. Now, once again, they lifted into flight to find the third and final point in the Devil's Triangle.

Ezylryb blinked as he perched on the limb of the spruce. Had he been dreaming or was what he felt real? It seemed to him that the buzz was dissipating and with it a fog of sorts was lifting from inside his head. He slowly spread his wings and swung his head to look in every direction. He almost felt as if he might be able to fly again with purpose and direction and not become muddled. Something was different. Perhaps he might try at least getting to another nearby tree. He should be able to do this without too much confusion. After all, he had been able to catch small prey that wandered directly beneath his tree. *Keep it simple,* he told himself. *Just keep your eye on that poplar over there. Focus on one branch. Lift off, then two wing beats and you're there. Concentrate. Meditate, the way the Glauxian brothers taught you so many years ago.*

Ezylryb was just about to lift off when he heard something flying noisily low to the ground.

"Ezylryb!" Gylfie cried out. "It's Ezylryb!"

He must be dreaming. It was the little Elf Owl, Soren's best friend. Then, overhead, he heard the unmistakable whistling sound of an owl with a coal in its beak. He sniffed the air. *The chaw is here!*

From a very high tree outside the triangle, an unusually large Barn Owl with a metal beak and mask covering half his face looked on in dismay as the owls burned the last bag of flecks and the snare was destroyed.

"Did you know, Your Pureness, that fire could do this to the sacred flecks?"

"Shut your beak." The High Tyto was tempted to rake

the vile owl with his talons, but with his other troops off in Kuneer, he needed all of his owls right now. There were six from the Great Ga'Hoole Tree, but there were ten of the Pure Ones. It was the Great Gray that would be their hardest foe. Now, of course, they had seven with the old one. But the old one was weak. He was weak but he was smart. And how close they had come to making him theirs. If they had only found a new castle, a fort, anything that the Others had left behind that could serve as their headquarters, they could have lured the Whiskered Screech there. As it was, they had had to stash him here and mind that enough game came his way so he wouldn't starve. He would do them no good dead. How valuable his knowledge would have been. With the old one, they would have not only dominated the Southern Kingdoms but the Northern ones as well, for that was where the old Screech came from — the land of the great North Waters, the land of the legendary warriors. And it was the old Screech who had probably taught them the trick with the fire. This owl had to be theirs. Throughout all the kingdoms of owls, this one — the one they called Ezylryb — or sometimes Lyze, was the most renowned. It was said that he possessed powers and knowledge that were unimaginable. The Pure Ones needed him. He might not be a Tyto but they needed him nonetheless. And they would get him. And once they got him they would crypt him and then they would truly possess him.

"Your Pureness, the Great Gray looks fierce. He might be a problem."

"A problem?" the High Tyto said slowly in a voice that frightened the Sooty Owl who had just spoken. "Has it escaped your notice, Wortmore, that these owls wear no battle claws?"

"That's right, sir. Never thought of that." Wortmore's voice quivered.

"Prepare to attack!"

Nine owls, all with heart-shaped faces, some dusky, some pure white, and one with a metal mask, unlocked the talons of their battle claws.

CHAPTER TWENTY

Attack!

Ezylryb stood with the two members of his chaw and the others in a circle on the ground as they watched the bag burn. As the last of the flecks glowed with an almost white heat, there was a feeling of great release. The chains that had bound the triangle had been broken and then it was as if the links of those chains had simply melted into the thin air of the night.

Soren was still reeling with disbelief. They had never in their wildest dreams expected to find Ezylryb smack in the middle of the Devil's Triangle.

"We should be able to get home by morning, before first light, I think," Soren finally said. He could barely speak, he was so filled with joy at the sight of his old ryb. Soren was just about to say that Digger could go on and bury this fire, that there was no need for coals, when suddenly the night ripped with the shrill screeches of owls.

"It's an attack!" Twilight cried and rose up huge, his talons extended. Soren saw there were ten owls, all with battle claws. And one with a metal beak was flying directly for Twilight. Twilight dodged in the nick of time. All Soren could think was, *We have no battle claws. We are only six, seven if you count Ezylryb. They'll rip us to shreds!* They would never survive.

Then, amazingly, ducking and dodging every parry from the oncoming Metal Beak, Twilight began one of his battle taunts.

> *You think those metal claws scare me.*
> *I'll clack my beak till you see three!*

The attacking owl almost stopped mid-flight. He was completely startled by this strange chant.

> *Your gizzard's soft as a worm*
> *I'm going to make you*
> *squirm, squirm squirm. . . .*

Twilight was filling the air with his hoarse, raucous rage. He was everywhere at once. He grabbed the mu shield they had been carrying and raised it just in time to catch a high blow from one of Metal Beak's claws. The battle claw raked through the soft metal of the shield but Twilight was protected nonetheless. The Great Gray Owl advanced. Soren, in the meantime, was dodging the battle claws of an angry-looking Sooty. But he was not sure how long he could keep this up. He could only dodge and fight defensively. He had nothing to attack with. Suddenly, a fiery spitting sound zinged through the forest. Had the red come come sizzling down to earth? Soren opened his eyes wide in sheer amazement. It was not the comet. It was Ruby with a burning coal in her mouth. *How did she find us?* And, unbelievably, Martin, his chaw buddy was close behind with a beakful of burning twigs. The odds were getting better. The sides more even with nine owls including Ezylryb from Ga'Hoole and ten followers of Metal Beak.

Ruby had ignited a branch of spruce and was flying with it in her talons, sweeping the air around her. There were still coals burning. Soren and Digger looked at each other and quickly grabbed whatever they could. They would attack. They could fight offensively and perhaps rout these owls. Otulissa joined in. In an instant, the air was whizzing with firebrands as the owls of the colliering chaw flew through the forest night. Gylfie and Eglantine kept the supply of firebrands coming as they dipped twigs and limbs into the coals. Soon, however, Gylfie and Eglantine discovered that they were not too small or too inexperienced to carry the slenderest of flaming striplings through the night to singe the underbellies of the enemy owls.

Deft and precise, the counterattack had begun in earnest. And all the time, Twilight's singsong gibes and jeers rang out through the forest, a jangling, blaring scornful taunt that distracted and struck fear into the Metal Beak's troops.

We got the fire, we got the punch,
we're gonna make you yarp your lunch.
One two three four five,
you're gonna wonder if you're alive.
Six seven eight nine ten,
you're as stupid as a big ole hen.
I can count forever and a day,
and maybe you better start to pray.

You call yourself pure,
the best owls in sight.
Well, you stink to high heaven,
and you ain't so bright.
You're stuck up as can be
and your gizzards can't handle milkberry tea.
You're no better than gull splat,
and even though you fly,
you're lower than a rat.

At that last verse, one of the Sooties was driven to such distraction that he flew straight into a burning branch that Ruby was holding. "Great Glaux!" the Short-eared Owl muttered. "I didn't have to even attack. He came right to me." The smell of singed feathers swirled in the air. Another one, who had been poked with a branch that had been ignited by a glowworm, flew off screaming.

But Metal Beak, undaunted, was advancing on Twilight in a rage that was deadly, his battle claws extended and glaring in the light of the flames. Ruby quickly slid in on Twilight's exposed flank, with her burning branch, and joined the battle against this large, horrifying owl. Soren and Otulissa advanced with flaming branches, slashing them like fiery swords at the other owls. One owl in Metal Beak's group went yeep and plunged to the ground. Immediately, Martin dropped a beakful of cinders on his flight feathers.

"I aimed for the eye," he breathlessly told Gylfie. "But I'm not nearly as good a marksman as Soren was with that bobcat."

"On your tail, Martin, watch it." A Sooty with claws extended raked out toward Martin's tail. With no thought of her personal safety, Gylfie dove into the heap of burning feathers of the owl who had gone yeep and came up with a wad in her mouth, trying to hold it just as she had seen the colliers hold the coals. Hurtling herself toward the owl that had attacked Martin, she spiraled upward and ignited his belly feathers. There was a terrific yowl and then the Sooty turned into an airborne burning missile on a wild trajectory. "Dodge! Eglantine!" Eglantine went into a lateral spiral, leaving a clear track for the missile that smashed headfirst into the trunk of a tree. The owl's battle claws had dropped off on the way. Soren swooped down and retrieved one. Otulissa the other.

"Together we might make a pair and do some damage!" Otulissa shouted to Soren.

"Twilight needs help! Get a burning branch." Eglantine flew up with a freshly ignited branch for Soren.

Otulissa had fearlessly flown ahead. *I've never flown with such big battle claws. Twilight should have these*, the thought raced through her head, but some instinct took over. She darted up and behind the huge owl, then plunged with the claws locked in the downward position and gave him a terrific blow. Metal Beak staggered mid-flight. He hadn't seen it coming, and now Soren flew up in a flanking maneuver and shoved the slender, burning stripling branch under the mask. He shoved harder and a great piece of the mask lifted and fell to the ground.

Soren blinked. He felt his heart stop, his gizzard turn to stone.

"Kludd!" The name boiled up from Soren's throat. His own brother now flew at him, his claws raised ready to rake out Soren's eyes.

"Surprise, little brother!" Soren dodged. His gizzard felt suddenly as if it was falling right out of him. Going yeep! Was he going yeep?

"He means to kill you, Soren!" It was Gylfie crying out, which brought him back to his senses. He dove for the still-burning branch. There was a thicker one beside it. He picked up that one instead and then, like a volcano spewing live embers that blistered the air, Soren rose to do battle with his brother. Extending his talons, one foot with the battle claw, the other with the fiery branch, he advanced on Kludd, who lurched forward in a feinting maneuver and then dove. Soren felt the air stir beneath him. Two seconds before, Kludd's battle claws would have raked his belly. Soren pivoted and flew straight up, an incredibly difficult maneuver but one that he executed perfectly. Kludd spun upward after him. But Soren could sense him before he saw him on his tail. Soren slowed his flight abruptly and plunged. Kludd overshot him, cursing all the while. Making a steeply banking turn to come back,

Kludd shouted down to Soren who was thirty feet or more below, "I'll get you!"

This was the hardest part. Soren had to hover — hover and not bolt and not go yeep! *Let him come, let him come. Steady, steady. Now!* Soren roared up underneath Kludd, holding the burning branch straight up. The embers landed on what little bit was left of the metal mask.

There was a deep grunt, followed by a quaking, horrendous scream. Then Ruby, Soren, and Twilight backed off and watched in a kind of hypnotic horror as the metal that had covered half the owl's face began to melt into a molten mass and spread across the entire face. Metal Beak's wings started to fold.

He's going yeep! Soren thought breathlessly. But then he blinked with disbelief as the owl, finding some extraordinary reserve of energy, raised his wings, twisted his head around, and opened the melting beak. "Death to the Impure. Long live Tytos supreme! Death to Soren! Turnfeather of the Pure, the true owls! Death to Soren!" The entire night seemed to sizzle with the words and then the enraged owl simply flew off into the night. Four owls were dead on the ground, the rest followed their leader, the Pure One with his beak still glowing red.

Suddenly, it was quiet. A singed feather drifted lazily

on a small night breeze. Soren perched on a branch. *My own brother. My very own brother is Metal Beak, and he wants to kill me. Kill me.* The forest, the world around him, seemed to dissolve. Soren felt as if he were alone in some weird space that was neither earth nor sky.

"Soren," Gylfie flew up and perched on the branch beside him. "Soren, you're going to be all right. Soren, he's crazy. It's what your mum's and da's scrooms were warning you about." Soren turned to the little Elf Owl. His eyes welled up with tears.

"But, Gylfie, there is still unfinished business on earth. He still lives. My parents' scrooms must still be far from glaumora."

"They're a little closer, Soren. They must be. They must be so proud of you. Look at what you have done."

Soren looked to a nearby branch on the same tree. All of his owls were safe, and there was Ezylryb perched on a lower branch with tears in his eyes as he looked at the young owls who had saved his life. But Soren was still seized by the terrible and overwhelming thoughts of Kludd. What Kludd had done to him and Eglantine, and what he, Soren, had done to Kludd. It was all simply too horrific to dwell on. So he turned his thoughts to something else — his best friend in the world, Gylfie. And she had just said that perhaps the scrooms of his parents were a little closer to glaumora. *Maybe, maybe,* he thought.

Soren looked down at Gylfie. How did she always know the right thing to say at the right time? But what about her own parents? Did she ever wonder if they were alive or dead? If they were scrooms between earth and glaumora?

"Gylfie," Soren said hesitantly. "Do you ever wonder about your parents?"

"Of course, Soren. But I think they're dead."

"But what if they aren't?"

"What do you mean?"

Soren was silent for a minute. He couldn't say what he really meant, for it was simply too selfish. If they were alive, it would mean that Gylfie would return to the Desert of Kuneer to live with them, and Soren didn't know if he could stand to lose the little Elf Owl.

"Oh, nothing," Soren answered and tried to make his voice sound light.

"Maybe someday we'll go to Kuneer and see. There's a spirit desert there, you know. If their scrooms are still around for unfinished business, that's where they would be."

"Yes, yes, I suppose so," Soren said quietly.

CHAPTER TWENTY-ONE

Good Light

Octavia slithered out on a limb of the great tree and scanned the sky. The night had grown thin, the black threadbare like a worn garment through which the first dim streaks of the morning would soon begin to glimmer. She had sensed that Soren and his little band would do something after she had discovered them in the secret chamber. Although she had not been born blind, she had grown to possess those extraordinary instincts and sensations of the other blind snakes. And now as Octavia slithered farther out onto the branch, she did sense something flying toward the tree. She coiled up and swung her head about. Something from far away was coming! Something was stirring the air. The vibrations seemed to ripple across her scales. Then she heard the lookout cry. "Owls two points north of east! Great Glaux! It's Ezylryb flying point! He's back! He's back!"

Tears began to stream from Octavia's sightless eyes. "He's coming back! He's coming back!" she whispered.

The Great Ga'Hoole tree began to shake with the sound of cheering owls. From every hollow, owls flew out — Snowies and Spotted Owls, Horned Owls and Great Grays, Elf and Pygmy Owls — to perch on the thousands of branches and cheer the return of the best of the best of the chaws and the greatest ryb of the great tree — Ezylryb.

As night faded into day, as Soren, Gylfie, Twilight, Eglantine, and Digger nestled into the down of their hollow, the clear music of the harp's strings began to slip through the branches of the great old tree. The voice of Madame Plonk so lovely, so eerily beautiful, as beautiful as the most distant stars, rose in the pale light. Soren heard the soft breathing of Eglantine beside him. He knew in a hollow high above theirs, Ezylryb was probably munching a caterpillar and perhaps, by the light of the fire in his grate, reading an old book. From the opening in their hollow, Soren could see the constellation of the Little Raccoon, its hind paw scratching the late autumn sky before it slipped off into another night in another world on another side of the earth. Madame Plonk's voice shimmered through the tree. Then he heard the loveliest liquid sound pour from the harp. It seemed to wrap them all in its music. He, of course, didn't know it but Octavia, old and fat as she was, had just jumped three octaves for the first time in years. She was so happy that she felt like a slim young thing again. She could almost see the notes as they floated out into the last darkness of the old night to touch the dawn.

"Good light," Soren said softly, and he said it seven times, for each of the owls he had led on their quest to mend a world that had been broken and to rescue a teacher who was loved.

"Good light," he said again. They were, however, all sound asleep.

In a hollow high up on the northwest side of the Great Ga'Hoole Tree, an old Whiskered Screech sat down at his writing table for the first time in months. He winced as he plucked a feather from his starboard wing. It always seemed that he grew his best quills on his starboard side for some reason. He then took out a new piece of his best writing parchment, dipped the quill into an inkwell, and began to write.

> *In a forest dark and tangled,*
> *smoke and fiery sparks did spangle*
> *the trees, the sky, the moon on high —*
> *it seemed as if Glaux did sigh.*

A Barn Owl with a metal face,
bellowed of his mighty race.
The chaw of chaws, did they cower
in what might be their final hour?
With their branches burning bright,
they tore into this evil night.
The flames danced across the mask —
a demon owl from Soren's past!

Nine others flanked him,
dark eyes so grim,
claws gleaming in the air,
set to rip, to stab, to tear.
So in that dark and tangled night,
the chaw of chaws rose to fight,
with talons bloodied, feathers singed.
A battle won — a war begins!

Ezylryb sighed deeply and put down his quill as the glare of the morning seeped into his hollow.

THE OWLS
and others
from
GUARDIANS *of* GA'HOOLE
The Rescue

SOREN: Barn Owl, *Tyto alba*, from the kingdom of the Forest of Tyto; snatched when he was three weeks old by St. Aegolius patrols; escaped from St. Aegolius Academy for Orphaned Owls

> His family:
> KLUDD: Barn Owl, *Tyto alba*, older brother
> EGLANTINE: Barn Owl, *Tyto alba*, younger sister
> NOCTUS: Barn Owl, *Tyto alba*, father
> MARELLA: Barn Owl, *Tyto alba*, mother

> His family's nest-maid:
> MRS. PLITHIVER, blind snake

GYLFIE: Elf Owl, *Micrathene whitneyi*, from the desert kingdom of Kuneer; snatched when she was almost three weeks old by St. Aegolius patrols; escaped from St. Aegolius Academy for Orphaned Owls; Soren's best friend

TWILIGHT: Great Gray Owl, *Strix nebulosa*, free flier, orphaned within hours of hatching

DIGGER: Burrowing Owl, *Speotyto cunicularius*, from the desert kingdom of Kuneer; lost in the desert after an attack in which his brother was killed and eaten by owls from St. Aegolius

ß   ß   ß

BORON: Snowy Owl, *Nyctea scandiaca*, the King of Hoole

BARRAN: Snowy Owl, *Nyctea scandiaca*, the Queen of Hoole

STRIX STRUMA: Spotted Owl, *Strix occidentalis*, the dignified navigation ryb (teacher) at the Great Ga'Hoole Tree

EZYLRYB: Whiskered Screech Owl, *Otus trichopsis*, the wise weather-interpretation and colliering ryb (teacher) at the Great Ga'Hoole Tree; Soren's mentor

POOT: Boreal Owl, *Aegolius funereus*, Ezylryb's assistant

MADAME PLONK: Snowy Owl, *Nyctea scandiaca*, the elegant singer of the Great Ga'Hoole Tree

OCTAVIA: Blind nest-maid snake for Madame Plonk and Ezylryb

DEWLAP: Burrowing Owl, *Speotyto cunicularius*, the Ga'Hoolology ryb at the Great Ga'Hoole Tree

BUBO: Great Horned Owl, *Bubo virginianus*, the blacksmith of the Great Ga'Hoole Tree

TRADER MAGS: Magpie, a traveling merchant

☙ ☙ ☙

OTULISSA: Spotted Owl, *Strix occidentalis*, a student of prestigious lineage at the Great Ga'Hoole Tree

PRIMROSE: Pygmy Owl, *Glaucidium californicum*, rescued from a forest fire and brought to the Great Ga'Hoole Tree the night of Soren's and his friends' arrival

MARTIN: Northern Saw-whet Owl, *Aegolius acadicus*, rescued and brought to the Great Ga'Hoole Tree the same night as Primrose; in Ezylryb's chaw with Soren

RUBY: Short-eared Owl, *Asio flammeus*, lost her family under mysterious circumstances and was brought to the Great Ga'Hoole Tree; in Ezylryb's chaw with Soren

SILVER: Lesser Sooty Owl, *Tyto multipunctata*, brought to the Great Ga'Hoole Tree after being rescued in the Great Downing

NUT BEAM: Masked Owl, *Tyto novaehollandia*, brought to the Great Ga'Hoole Tree after being rescued in the Great Downing

ß   ß   ß

THE ROGUE SMITH OF SILVERVEIL: Snowy Owl, *Nyctea scandiaca*, a blacksmith not attached to any kingdom in the owl world

---

About the Author

KATHRYN LASKY lives in Cambridge, Massachusetts, with her husband. She is the author of several books, which include the Guardians of Ga'Hoole, Wolves of the Beyond, and Daughters of the Sea series.